T0113448

Acclaim for

Irini Spanidou's **God's Snake**

"*God's Snake . . .* is at once austere and rich, hallucinatory and direct, humorous, and profoundly disturbing."
—*Washington Post Book World*

"Brilliant. . . . [It] has something of the hard simplicity of a Greek myth." —Doris Lessing

"Magical, absorbing, most original. . . . This marvel of a book brilliantly conveys the mercurial moods that afflict childhood, and that old theme of growing up seems fresh and vital again."
—*People*

"This is a remarkable work, clear, direct, truthful."
—Grace Paley

"Irini Spanidou's writing, rich in detail, conveys a striking sense of time and place. Her remembered Greece is fascinating. *God's Snake* is a splendid book." —Robert Stone

"Irini Spanidou's story of a child growing up in a world of beauty mixed with cruelty is an old one; that you read it like something you've never read before is the best testimony of the remarkable art of the author." —Josef Skvorecky

"I read *God's Snake* with great delight and gratitude. It really *is* a wonderful book—passionate and fearless." —Alice Munro

ALSO BY IRINI SPANIDOU

Fear

Irini Spanidou
God's Snake

Irini Spanidou is the author of *Fear*.
She lives in New York City.

INTERNATIONAL

God's Snake

I r i n i   S p a n i d o u

Vintage International
Vintage Books
A Division of Random House, Inc.
New York

Library of Congress Cataloging-in-Publication Data
Spanidou, Irini.
God's snake / Irini Spanidou.
p.   cm.
ISBN 978-0-375-70286-0
I. Title.
PS3569.P354G63   1999
813'.54—dc21   98-18170
CIP

www.randomhouse.com

146694632

For my grandmother, Irini Hatzinikoli

Snakes

THE FIRST SNAKE I saw was dead and so were those of a long time after, but that first snake my father brought home and threw at my feet saying, "A dead snake." His orderly Manolis picked it up with some tongs and carried it out of the house, and I went back to my homework. It was an unusual occurrence, but that would be that, I thought. Not so. Manolis came home a few days later carrying a burlap sack in his hand, which he tossed to and fro. He stood inside the door of the house like someone who has important news to announce.

"I got a snake for you," he said.

"Another one?"

"Different kind."

"Dead?"

"Dead."

Keeping the head inside the sack because, he said, it was bashed, he let the rest of it out and dangled it in front of him like a long tail, trying to make it wiggle the way one does with a piece of rope. The snake corpse had no bounce. It hung straight down, limp and soggy like something drowned.

It didn't interest me. How could I be interested in a species whose head I could not see? As if Mrs. Fotiou were to put paper bags over the heads of animals she showed us in class and say: "Coyote . . . Hyena . . . Muskrat. . . ."

I wasn't interested in zoology anyway. Studying the genealogy and private habits of an animal lost me. My mother, on the other hand, pored over my natural history textbooks and read with delight down to the footnotes. So many vertebrae. So many fins. She stared transfixed at the pictures.

"Look at that! . . . Ah, Nature," she'd say.

The more exotic the animal, the greater her excitement and pleasure. I was too close to childhood still, and it was all wonder and no wonder to me. I made no distinction between things great and small. The sight of a rooster crowing at dawn, puffed up as though the sun rose at his command, or of gorillas pounding their chests in a rage of bliss was equally strange and equally acceptable to me. There was magic or there was no sense. If a worm cut in half lives, werewolves exist, I thought. I looked at animal pictures with a certain respect, polite and congenial, the way I looked at pictures of relatives of friends when they were singled out in the family album and the friend said, "Uncle Yannis as a recruit in the Balkan Wars . . . Cousin Loula at her christening . . . Antonis before he lost his toes in the boating accident," and such. I nodded at people I did not—and could or *would* not—know, some long since dead or otherwise departed—most likely to America or Australia, making their fortunes and leading lives different from ours. Nevertheless, I said, looking at them, "Uncle Yannis! Imagine! . . . Ah! Loula! . . . Antonis!" Similarly, "The kinkajou. *Potos flavus.* Hmm . . . The mongoose. *Dologate dybowskii.* Ha!" I gave them no more thought.

Still, my father insisted I learn all I could learn about the ways of nature and in bivouacs his men were instructed to capture any animal that came their way dead or alive. What mostly came their way was snakes. Snakes and more snakes that Manolis brought for me to see. Neither he nor I liked the ordeal, but my father ordered it. And, if some chap had to polish his boots with eighty strokes bellowing "one two three four . . ." while his company at ease looked on, and he, Manolis, had to amass dead snakes and present them to the major's daughter, such was the army and such was his luck. Unlike me, Manolis was resigned.

As he didn't know the snakes' proper names, he gave me the nicknames for the ones popular in that region but which, like a.k.a.'s of small-time crooks, varied from place to place, only "The Viper" being called "The Viper" all over Greece. There was "Yellow Spot," "Silver Frock," "Death Potion," and the nondescript, commoner type referred to as "Snakey." Letting the tail end of the snake out of the sack, he said without looking at me,

"Such and Such."

"Bad?"

"Killer."

Or: "Such and Such."

"Bad?"

"I wouldn't step on it."

Or: "Such and Such."

"Bad?"

"B-a-a-d."

That was the full extent of my instruction.

Once I asked him if he buried the bodies.

"That's why my mother bore me," he said. "To bury snakes."

I gathered burying them was inappropriate or uncustomary or maybe demeaning somehow and didn't press him with questions. I started asking my parents' friends, "Do dead snakes stink?" "Did you ever bury a snake?" "What happens to a snake after it dies?"

One Sunday afternoon in the officers' club the brigadier general beckoned me over.

"I hear you are interested in snakes."

Having questions about something is not the same as being interested in it, I thought. But I said, "Yes, sir. I am, sir." I was not allowed to contradict him.

The first time I met him, he said, "You look just like your mother."

"No, I don't," I said. "I look like my father. He spit to make me, Mommy says."

"Anna, you were impertinent," my mother said later.

"Why?"

"One does not disagree with higher rank. Neither does one talk about oneself, unless specifically asked, and then it's 'yes, sir' and 'yes, sir' and 'yes, sir,' no matter what you're told."

My father was silent.

"You mean I should lie?"

"It's not lying," said my father. "It's obedience."

"And when the man is wrong?"

"You obey the rank, not the man, Anna. And when he says to you, 'Donkeys fly,' you say, 'Donkeys fly, sir.'"

"Why?"

"Because when he says, 'You are the man to die,' you say, 'Yes, sir,' and you go and die."

"Oh, dying! We're not talking about dying. We're talking about donkeys flying. I'd die before I said, 'Donkeys fly.'"

"You'd say it," he said. "You'd say it and you'd dance a jig to the tune if I had my hands on you."

"I want to be a hero."

"Heroes don't make good soldiers."

"They win wars!"

"No, they do not. Soldiers win wars. Hundreds and thousands of nameless, dead soldiers. The heroes *I*'ve known were rascals—rascals who got lucky."

"In history—"

"History is books. The army is not heroism. The army is duty."

"So I'm to lie?"

"To obey. Obey till the time comes to command. Say to

yourself: 'Don't ever forget the taste of the dirt you were made to eat. Don't ever become what—under the boot—you hated and despised,' and you'll be a good leader, a good army man. The rest is drums and fanfare."

It's not only being in the army but being born to it that has its effects.

This much said about the spirit of obedience, back to the brigadier general.

"You like snakes, huh?"

"Yes, sir."

"You're an unusual little girl."

"Yes, sir."

"I have a little something to show you."

"Not another snake, sir! I mean—yes? A snake, sir?"

He smiled.

"Right now, sir?"

"If you would."

The brigadier general lived in the upper floor at the officers' club. He was married but his wife did not follow him to the provinces. He was of slight build, shortish, with beautiful but unimposing features, and there was a nervousness in his bearing that made him look conceited, not proud; defiant, not self-assured. Though there was no authority in his step, he had an aura of conferred power about him, the confidence of inherited privilege. His father and grandfather had both been generals in the Greek army, and his mother was a lady-in-waiting to the queen. When he made his appearance at a social gathering, he walked with the austere loneliness of a man following a hearse, and greeted those to the left and right with slight head inclinations and uncommunicative eyes. Revelry was suspended and, momentarily, all joy in life. We parted like the Red Sea waters to let him pass while some toady said in hushed and awed tones, "His mother is a lady-in-waiting . . . His mother is a lady-in-waiting . . ."

His name was Phaedon Dimitriadis and he didn't social-
ize with anyone privately. In conversation with my father,
my mother said once that he was neurasthenic but a fine man
even so, and my father called him a "butter-ass boy," irrevo-
cably closing the matter.

I had no opinion of my own. I did not know what "neurasthenic" meant. "Butter-ass boy" was more evocative but not
clear enough in my mind. I was curious.

On the way to his room I wondered how the snake had
been taken to him. Not in a burlap sack for sure, I thought. I
imagined everything involving a general would be done
according to rule and protocol, and burlap did not seem official. Maybe the snake would be in a box. Or on a special
stretcher. And maybe I could see the whole body then.
Finally see a head!

But when we got to his room there was no snake around
and all the general had to show me was a big, long painting.

"You know what that is?" he said.

"A painting. A modern painting."

"No, no, no. Look closer."

I looked closer. "It's framed snake skin, sir."

"Do you like it?"

"Yes, sir. I do. It's nice."

"I've always had this," he said. "I've taken it with me
wherever I've gone. I've had it with me throughout the war."

Thinking the general was then on active duty, I imagined
him carrying the framed snake skin with him and hanging it
up in the trenches. His face was beatific with excitement.

How can he be so excited over something that's always
been his? I thought. Over a piece of skin? He looked at me
expectantly as though I should be jumping up and down,
clapping my hands. He was truly crazy—and all the crazier
in assuming I was crazy, too.

I avoided his eyes, embarrassed.

"I haven't seen this variety yet," I said.

The snake skin looked like a mosaic of rubies, emeralds, amethysts and slivers of glimmering amber inlaid in steel, forming irregular circles and stripes—unlike any snake skin I'd seen before and, lacquered as it was, unlike leather.

"You couldn't have. It comes from South America. The snakes in Greece are nothing to speak of."

I was cut to the quick. I couldn't bear it when another country had something bigger or better than Greece. Even our snakes I didn't want to fall short. Especially our snakes, I felt just then.

"You mean 'nothing to speak of' regarding looks?"

I wasn't going to yes-sir him. This was a patriotic matter. To my surprise, he laughed.

"You mustn't judge by looks," I said. "Our snakes are shrewder. They are the sliest."

"Lowliest, sneakiest, meanest—worst of them all."

I was abashed.

"I wish," I said, "Greece was the way it used to be."

"Ah, child . . ."

"I believe we'll be great again. Do you?"

"I'm a little cynical."

"What's cynical?"

"You'll know when you grow up."

"Do you know the one difference between myself and my father?"

"No. What?"

"Dad is not ashamed of us. He doesn't even care we don't measure up. We are true men, he says. We have nobility and greatness in our hearts. He says, what is past is past. But I want us to be glorious, like in the books."

"Ah, child . . ." he said again. "Come close."

I went up to him and stood at attention in the appropriate distance.

He shook his head and smiled and looked at me in startled curiosity as though he'd never seen my face before, as
though we hadn't just been talking of snakes and things.

"You're a strange child," he said.

I'm strange? I thought. *You're* strange.

I walked around the room inspecting the things in it.
There wasn't much. The snake skin on the wall over a cot
covered with regulation blankets. A map of Greece on the
opposite wall. An armoire. A chair with a standing lamp and
an ashtray-spittoon alongside it. A desk completely bare. A
bookcase with wood-paneled doors.

"General, you have books?"

He took a key out of his pocket and opened the bookcase
for me. It was full.

"Oh, general! General! May I borrow one?"

"These are not for children."

"Poetry then."

"You understand poetry?"

"What's there to understand? It's beautiful—I love it."

"Beauty makes us love—ugliness makes us think. That's
how it is, isn't it?"

Did ugliness make me think? Everything made me think,
I thought. I didn't say anything.

"Later, beauty will make you think, that it exists at all
will make you think, and ugliness will make you love—will
make you need to love. To protest ugliness you'll love."

He *is* strange, I thought. "Me?"

"That's the kind of woman you'll be when you grow up."

"I'm not going to be a woman when I grow up."

"How old are you?" he asked.

"Ten."

He shook his head, looked at me silently for a long time,
then walked over to the window and turned his back to me.

The general's body had the sad grace of a sapling that has

aged without growing to be a tree. It was supple, beaten soft by suffering. As he leaned against the window frame his back curved, expressing the feelings banished from his face: longing, tenderness, fear, sadness—the cleavage between the shoulderblades like a crease of pain.

I love him, I felt suddenly. I love this general.

As though guessing my thoughts, he turned and looked at me. My heart tightened, my hands sweated and my feet froze. I couldn't look at him. I didn't love him. No, I thought. It can't be. But he turned his back to me again and my heart beat fast and warmth spread over me and I felt I loved him once more. As he stayed facing away and as I looked at his back, my love grew and grew and it was as though it made roots on the spot where I was and I couldn't move—could not leave the room and could not go up to him but stood where I stood and thought I would have to stand there forever. I was frightened.

"Remember when I said you looked like your mother?"

"Yes."

He was still looking out the window and talking as though to someone outside.

"You do. You have your mother's smile. We are like the person whose smile we take after. Remember that sometime. Don't go thinking you're like your father."

"I like my father," I protested.

He turned around. "I see you do," he said.

"Who do *you* look like?"

"My mother."

"Who do you smile after?"

"No one. Nobody."

Whom does he take after then? I thought. He's unique! A phenomenal general.

I was proud, I was thrilled to be in love with him, but it was upsetting to love him when his back was turned and feel fear and shame when he faced me. As he looked at me now I wished I could melt into my shoes. Then my shoes would swell and become heavy and big like a giant's and go *clump clump clump* with nothing anyone could see in them and I'd vanish.

"Sir. I must go," I said.

"If you must, Little Ponytail."

He gave me a leatherbound copy of the poems of Drosinis, said I could keep it, and kissed the top of my head.

"General, sir. Now that we're friends . . . I don't *really* like snakes."

"No?"

"No."

"I didn't *really* think you did. Dismissed, sweet."

As I walked home, the image of the general kept coming into my mind and I saw him the way one sees things in dreams, an inner vision that displaced the outer though my eyes were open. I was startled. I started running. I stopped to catch my breath and ran and stopped and ran till I got home in a panic. I couldn't understand what had happened to me.

My hands were hot. I felt love in my hands. They were trembling. It was in happiness they were trembling. My heart beat fast. It was in fear it beat fast. Though the general was far away, I felt as though he were near me and it was as though the book in my hands, the book he had given me, felt my touch and took in my love becoming magic.

I stood in the middle of my room, head stooped, completely still.

"What are you doing in the dark?" my mother asked when she and my father got home.

"Thinking."

She turned on the light and saw the book in my hands. "What is this?"

"General Dimitriadis gave it to me."

"Did you say thank you?"

"No."

"I told you a thousand—"

"Did you ask him for it?" my father said from the hall.

"Yes."

"You shouldn't ask for things, Anna. If you don't have pride, at least have manners."

I sat at the edge of my bed. I felt worthless. Guilty, too. This love is wrong, I thought. My father hates, he despises, the general. I could feel it from his voice, the darkness that passed his eyes when he spoke his name. He was the opposite of the general.

My father was tall, dark, muscular, handsome, fierce. He looked everyone in the eyes, even women and children. His voice never wavered. His questions were implied commands, his orders firm, quietly spoken statements. He did not desire or elicit servile obedience but manful acceptance of one's duty to do what must be done. He looked at his men with esteem and made them feel—as though it were trust— they'd be beneath contempt to betray it. You were good or you were no good at all in his eyes. You were a man or you were not a man. As a soldier you were his pawn but in your humanity you were his and everyone else's equal—an army egalitarianism he practiced and believed in as he believed in the cause of the army, its function in society, its service in turning youths into men going out in the world as though reborn, passed through a new womb to adult life. When privates walked out of the barracks gates for the last time, stunned to be free, blinking in the sun, their gait uncertain, their old civilian clothes crumpled, ill-fitting, sagging like shedding skin, he watched from his office window wistfully. He loved his men. Years later they fell in his arms when by chance they saw him on the street, crying, "My captain, sir! . . . My lieutenant, sir! . . . My major, sir!" according to what his rank had been when they passed through his hands. They hugged him and tears came to their eyes. He is like a father to them, I thought. They are like brothers to me. It was as though I had thousands and thousands of brothers all over Greece.

Whenever I saw a man I liked, I asked him:

"Were you in the army?"

What man had *not* in the years right after the war!

"Did you serve under my father?"

If the answer was no, I was mistrustful and disappointed.

My father was wonderful, I thought. The whole world adored him. I wanted to be just like him.

Maybe I'd grow to be someone just like my father and marry someone just like the general. That might settle it.

"WHAT DOES CYNICAL mean?" I asked my mother at the table.

"Where did you hear that word?"

"General Dimitriadis said he was cynical."

"The general told you he was cynical?"

She was incredulous. I wasn't sure if she disbelieved that the general would say such a thing or that he could be what the word meant.

"A *little* cynical."

"He gives the child a book of sentimental drivel and tells her he's cynical," she said to my father.

"A cynic," he said, "is someone who believes man is a dog and deserves a dog's life."

"If she's going to learn something, let her learn it right."

"So, what's a cynic?" he said.

"Someone who lives without hopes, dreams and lies," my mother said.

Immediately I imagined someone very thin, with sallow skin, big circles under his eyes and dry lips. Not the general *at all*. Maybe "a little" cynical, like parsimony of the spirit, meant allowing yourself so many dreams, so many hopes, and so many lies just to get by. That *could* be him and it upset me, as I myself was a person of enthusiasm and hope.

"That's not a cynic," my father said, however. "It may have been Diogenes, but it's not a cynic."

"Who's Diogenes?"

They ignored me.

"It's a cynic, properly speaking," my mother said.

"Properly speaking it's someone who ascribes his own baseness to others," he said.

"Who's Diogenes?" I repeated.

"A philosopher who was a cynic. In ancient Greece, in Korinth—"

"Oh, for Christ's sake," my father interrupted.

"If we have something to give our children it's history."

"History won't feed them and history won't clothe them."

"In Korinth . . ." my mother went on.

To hear her tell it, Diogenes was wild. I was amazed. I laughed so hard even my father smiled. Cynic or no cynic, Diogenes was a philosopher after my heart. I liked the story of the barrel and the featherless biped and the lantern in the night, but most of all I liked his meeting with Alexander, how Alexander asked Diogenes if there was anything he'd like from him and Diogenes said: "Yeah. Step aside a ways. You're blocking the sun." What pluck! I thought. It made me admire Diogenes boundlessly on the spot. Even so, there was no doubt who of the two I'd like to be. Alexander, of course! If only I had lived then . . .

"Now," said my father. "What's cynical?"

"Not having ambition?" I said.

"No. It's cynical to think that people *with* ambition are fools."

This explanation satisfied all three of us.

Later, in bed, I thought of a cow I had seen.

Manolis and I had been crossing the field that lay between the barracks and the village, when we saw a white-spotted cow. She turned her head, eyes glazed with wonder and benevolence, looked up at us like a myopic without glasses, then went back to grazing. A serious animal, I thought. Manolis, who never relaxed from his sense of duty, pointed to her and said, "A cow!" Just as he said it, the cow fell on her side with a thud, sprawled on her back and stayed with her legs up. She wants to be tickled, I thought.

"Look," I said. "A cow that wants to be petted."

"She's dead," Manolis said.

We went close and stood by the carcass with our heads bent like two people by a grave. She had been my first dead cow—my first dead animal other than a snake—and I was beside myself with interest. Manolis' eyes were downcast but empty of funereal solemnity. He was looking at his combat boots, the toes curling up, the uppers rising like dough gone haywire. He must be worrying about his toes, I thought, the way I worry about my fingers when I wear mittens and spread them and twist them and try to count them to make sure they're all there.

As he saw me watching him, he looked up and said, with no more ceremony than he'd use referring to a missed bus:

"Gone!"

The cow was becoming stiff as though clenching her body in fear. There was an awful look in her eyes. I followed her stare but saw nothing. What she sees, I thought, must be in death, not in life. It must be something horrible, something dreadful—it's terrifying her. And she can't close her eyes. The dead can't close their eyes. But their eyes must see, like hair and nails that grow in the grave, eyes must continue to see, and what they see fills them with terror, a terror they're locked in forever, forever they're dead.

I thought of all the bad people and criminals and those who were hanged or died unjustly—murdered or killed in wars—with no one to close their eyes. Their death must be like living an eternity in fear, the same unchanging fear. That must be hell, I thought. The thought horrified me. It was much more vivid and clear than my thoughts of paradise which came to me all in grayish hazy colors and indistinct shapes when I imagined it, as though the other world was a foggy place and the air tepid—people's souls milling, dragging about, the feeling like Sunday afternoons when the family meal is over, the older relatives doze in their chairs and children are too bored to play. I was unsettled. Maybe, I thought, if only you close your eyes, death is like nothing.

"Manoli, do you believe in the Second Coming?"

"Yes."

"I can't understand how eternity won't have an end. I'd much rather it did."

"Eternity doesn't end. It's how eternity is."

"I won't like it."

Manolis shrugged.

I did not question how the dead would rise—I believed in the trumpets and the graves opening up and God sitting on His throne. It was what happened after the dead rose that puzzled me. What then? I became sick with worry when priests said bright-eyed: ". . . and life everlasting. Amen." This no-end notion rattled my mind. I didn't want to be resurrected if I could help it. Now this cow with that look in her eye made me not want to ever be dead.

I nudged Manolis' sleeve and we started home, leaving the dead cow behind. Manolis was walking fast to make up for the time we'd wasted and I had to follow at a trot to keep up with him. It's hard to have grave thoughts when your feet have to hurry. By the time we got home, the cow was just a story to tell.

"I saw a dead cow, Ma."

"Not when I'm cooking, Anna."

"I saw a dead cow, Ma."

"Not when we're eating, Anna."

"I saw a dead cow, Ma."

"Your father and I are talking, Anna."

So I never told it.

I couldn't go to sleep. After the dead cow, the dead snakes came to my mind. I wondered about their heads, why it was they were always missing. It must be the only way to kill them, I thought. Must be their heart is in their head—they have no chest to keep it. Their heart must be in their head for sure or it'd have to be anywhere along the body, as though God closed His eyes after He made them and where His hand stopped there, He decided, the heart would go.

How could the general *like* snakes? As their heart went tick tick, tick tick inside their brain, they couldn't possibly feel it, they couldn't even hear it, I thought. All they must think is: "I am. I am. I want. I want." No wonder they crawl. It's our heart that makes us look an animal in the eye and say as though hearing its own heart beat, "you're like us—you have heart," and love it and want to hug it. Who'd want to hug a snake or even touch one? Unlike the cow's, their corpse is not disquieting. The wonder about snakes is that they exist at all, that their life begins, not that it ends. Suddenly the snake Manolis had shown me that morning appeared behind my eyes, wiggling and winking inside my head as if saying, "But it *doesn't* end. I looked dead but I wasn't. Snakes don't die. Here I am, see?" The image faded, then came back. Wiggle. Wiggle. Wink. Wink. Faded, then came back. I sat up.

"I don't want a snake in my head, God," I said. "What *is* this?"

It's strange of the general to like snakes, I thought. And it's strange of me to like a strange general.

MY FEELINGS HAD not changed the next day. I still loved the general. I read Drosinis' *Poems* as though the general himself had written them—and written them for me—and after I had read them, read them again. I read the book all day.

"Those who know books don't know life. And those who know life don't know books," said my father contemptuously.

"Do you understand that you're a child?" said my mother. "Play. There's still light out. I *said,* go out and play."

She snatched the book from my hands and locked it in her vanity among her jewelry, powder and lipsticks.

Banished to the garden, I sat on a crate with my hands on my knees. My mother watched from the window above. She hates me, I thought.

Army children have distinctive marks: a stiffness in their bearing, a solemnity that—unlike the false gravity of the officers—is abused innocence, submerged melancholy. They have the self-esteem and -reliance of children whose parents have or represent power, but in their reserve there's a solitary's wariness of others. They are hated strangers in every new place—the military is an occupying force always. Outposts are lonely. But for the children there isn't even the regularity and conformity of barracks life. They are outsiders in a small village or town, new kids in school who have to claim and defend their ground then abandon it and move on.

It was a hard life for me. I was lonesome. Other children were close to their mothers. My own would rather I hadn't been born. She liked to tell how she hadn't wanted to marry my father, how she hadn't wanted to bear me.

I came out between her legs rejected by her whole body like something foreign, that had been implanted. When they took me to her washed and clothed and put me in her arms, she held me as though they had handed her an unjust sentence. She was eighteen, unhappy, foolish and vain in her girlishness, years away yet from loving. Like a wild animal caged when young, she had the brooding vehemence of unrealized strength, a peeved sadness.

She was beautiful, with deep green eyes and jet black hair that she wore loose, shoulder length, in untidy waves around the house and pulled back in a bun when she went out, looking severe, uncondescending, prim but for her stride, which was fast, insinuatingly lithe. Men turned around to look at her and women eyed her with dislike. She had no friends.

We lived as though we were camping, the furniture minimal, essential, the folding kind—simple props like a road company's. But my mother wouldn't make believe as we set up house every few months and played at mother, father and child that she had a family. She acted as though she did not belong with us, as though caught in our life by circumstance, and it was the same misery always. When I came upon her unexpected and she was in the house alone, I found her sitting in a chair, stooped, her face in her hands, sobbing. I felt then that I was seeing something I shouldn't, something forbidden a child to see. I felt I'd done wrong. To be there. To see her crying. To be myself at all. I went near, put my arms around her shaking back and said, "Mommy . . . Mommy . . ." But worse than pushing me away, she said nothing and stayed rigid and cold in my arms, and after a while, got up and closed herself in her room and did not come out again till dark.

She opposed my father in everything—his ideas, tastes, wishes—acted as though she had no regard for his needs, yet gave in to his advances, her body taunting in its taut passivity, lazy, arching like a cat's under a petting hand, her eyes cold, imperious as my father's were hot, imploring. When he bent to kiss her on the shoulder near the neck, he put his fingers through her hair whispering he loved her in a soft, tender voice as though the harshness and contempt he had for her now disappeared. She looked away, a glint in her eyes part malice part pleasure, a vengeful triumph betrayed in the corners of her smile as he said, "My love . . . sweet love . . . I love you . . ."

If I looked like her, I thought, she'd like me, she'd love me. But she didn't see herself in me. Except as a moral responsibility she did not own up to my existence and, when we were left alone, she avoided my eyes.

It was as though I'd sprung out of my father's head like Athena from the head of Zeus, as though I was entirely my father's child. When I was born, he made the sign that signifies "cunt," touching and stretching the forefingers and thumbs of his hands, announcing I was female with a leer, and went out to get drunk with his men. But as he saw his own features setting on my small face, my eyes dark and haunted—the eyes of an infant still seeing the darkness of the womb, that haven't smiled yet—something tightened in his heart and changed in his mind, and he loved me. His love was a proud, selfish love, the love he had for himself, as though I was his flesh, his image, his self remade.

If I disappointed him, he said, "What kind of man are you?" I cringed in my skin, mortified. What kind of man was I? A bad one obviously. An inferior kind.

Or, worse, he said: "You're acting like a woman! Get away from me!" I thought being a woman was a character defect—like being a swindler or a quack. If someone were to say it was connected to my "pee-pee," I'd look down at myself astounded and think, are they crazy? My genitals were like my nose and tongue to me. Everybody had them, I thought.

What of it? My genitals were just fine. It was my mind that wasn't quite right, the propensity to act like a woman lurking treacherously inside it, raising its head at the most unexpected and inopportune moments, much like the urge to stand on my head in the middle of a gathering when I was the only child there and the grown-ups bored me.

"If you want to act like an idiot, act like an idiot," my father said calmly at such times.

I got back to my heels and, slowly, unrepentingly, I left the room. That much leeway he gave me. But to act like a woman, oh no! Never!

He set out to reform me and forced science and math on me to toughen my mind—make it strong and incisive like a man's. I resisted. I liked my mind soft and pliable. Thoughts sank into it pell-mell, unformed, and came out of it full-fledged, incontestably clear. I am *what* and *how* I think, I thought. That my father disapproved made me feel wronged.

I did my extra homework with a sense of outrage. I did not like science. There were, of course, those who did and that was fine for them, I guessed. My cousin Lakis from Athens, who was my age and did chemical experiments, once burned the lashes off his eyes while the family had gotten together in his house for Shrove Monday. He repeated the experiment with swimming goggles and his mother's skiing gloves which, in the new explosion, dissolved to bits giving off a stink that made us stiffen our backs and shift in our chairs alarmed and incredulous at the odious, undefinable smells that emanated from the corridor. Aunt Louisa passed a chocolate box saying with a candid and earnest face that the ones with praline had much to recommend them but we should stay away from those filled with cherries.

"What *is* that, Louisa?" asked Grandpa Damien, sniffing the air.

"I don't know, Father," said Aunt Louisa.

"It's Lakis in the bathroom," Cousin Mary said.

"Stavro!" Aunt Louisa called to my uncle as if afraid to move. "The child!"

"He's got parasites, the poor youngster," concluded Aunt Vasilia. She was sickness-minded. "Enemas are the thing, Louisa. Trust me."

Aunt Louisa was dumbfounded.

"It's no good giving him tablets," Aunt Vasilia went on. "Modern methods are hogwash. Flush him out, I say."

Cousin Mary got in front of Aunt Vasilia and looked her sternly in the eye. She was fourteen, bookish, had protruding eyes and put her nose everywhere. She lisped but spoke with moral certitude and *very* correctly.

"There's nothing wrong with Lakis' intestines, Mother," she said. "He's not e-v-a-c-u-a-ting. He's in the bathroom doing chemical experiments."

"Chemical experiments!"

We were all on our feet. By then a loud, pounding noise was coming from the end of the hall and Uncle Stavros' shouting, "Open the door! Open the door or I'll break it!" and then a huge crash. The door broke off the hinges and landed on the floor with Uncle Stavros face down, still pounding on it.

Lakis sat on the bathtub rim shaking bits of burned glove off bleeding fingers, his eyes behind the goggles intense and unblinking like a big, sad fish's. He stared at us impervious to our shock as though doing experiments in bathrooms was like blowing your nose into old socks or drinking your milk with a spoon—simply idiosyncratic.

He took the goggles off and we saw the burns around his eyes.

"Laki!" we screamed.

"Idiot!" cried Uncle Stavros scrambling to his feet. "I'll kill you!"

Aunt Louisa tried to stop him but he pushed her to the wall.

"Get away!" he said. "All of you, get away. I'll kill him!"

Grabbing him by the back of the shirt and dragging him to the yard, he beat him with the hose while the rest of us ran to the veranda and watched, the children bending over the railing, the grownups standing back.

"Will you do it again?" said Uncle Stavros every time he raised the hose.

"Yes," said Lakis without crying.

"Will you do it again?"

"Yes."

"Will you do it again?"

"Yes."

Finally Uncle Stavros' anger was spent.

Chin up, hips swaying, Lakis went and sat in a wheelbarrow in the lot next door. We—all the young cousins—ran to be with him. We didn't know about chemical experiments but we knew about guts. Lakis was a hero—he was our trophy. We rolled him in the wheelbarrow around the house that was being built, cheering. Then we wanted our own ride.

"My turn . . . My turn . . ." each one said.

Lakis sat on the fence and licked the burns on his hands. He wasn't much for company and games.

"I'm sorry the experiment failed," I told him.

"Failed? How do you mean failed? It nearly blew my hands off!"

"It wasn't accidental?"

"What wasn't?"

"The accident."

"It wasn't an accident, I tell you. Next time you can be in on it, if you want."

Did he mean I could have my hands blown off too if I wanted?

"My problem is flooring," he said.

"Flooring?"

"Mama has a thing about her floors. Her rugs . . . her parquet . . . the marble tiles . . . the brick tiles . . . the mosaic. . . . Where can I work? Where? I need a place to stand."

Just like when Archimedes propounded the theory of levers, I thought.

"Give me a place to stand and I'll move the earth," I said.

He didn't get it.

"Archimedes."

"Ah," he said, "levers! Moving the unmovable. . . . Ancient stuff. It's 'destroying the indestructible' now."

"The atomic bomb?"

"The atomic bomb leaves matter. The thing is to make nothing. Real nothing."

"Then what?"

"Then nothing. *Nothing* nothing."

"What interests *me* is infinity. It isn't that it interests me so much as that it bothers me. Does it bother you?"

"No. Why should it?"

"For me it's like my mind goes in loops and I can't stop it. A dizziness that's shaped like a funnel—it starts here and goes to here," I pointed on myself, "spins in my head and swallows all my thoughts except 'infinity' 'infinity' 'infinity' and I get a tingling behind my nose and I think I'll faint."

"Weird."

"Then I think, 'I'm Anna . . . I'm Anna . . . I'm Anna . . . ,' and it goes away."

"Weird."

"When I think of infinity . . . and eternity . . . and how the

world began, what came before the beginning and before
that and before that—"

"You're philosophical," he cut in. "I'm physical."

"Who says I'm not physical?"

"Physical as in physics. Philosophical as in philosophy. If
you stop being philosophical you'll be all right. I mean, you
won't be having spells and things."

"But I don't want to be philosophical. It comes over me
suddenly. I can be blowing on my soup and it hits me."

"Maybe you are crazy."

"I *am* not."

"Nothing hits *me* when I blow on *my* soup."

"And *I* don't get my face and my hands busted."

"I don't mind getting them busted. I *like* getting them
busted. 'Scars are a soldier's true medals.' "

"And what do *you* know about soldiers?"

"I'm a boy."

"Ha!"

"You wanna see?"

"No."

"I'll show it to you if you wanna see it."

"You showed it to me last week."

"I will again . . ."

"No."

"Why did you come talk to me?"

"Not because I wanted to see your thing. Big deal."

"Who's talking!"

I hit him and he hit me and we fell on the ground and tore
and scratched at each other and parted sworn enemies.

Whenever we talked after that, Lakis examined what I
said as though suspecting me of things devious and batty.
We did not smile as we spoke. Our eyes met and got glazed
and glassy. He lowered his eyes to my feet then raised them
slowly over my body to my neck as though contemplating

the mystery of my organism, how he could get to the bottom of it. The look made me restless. I felt a deep unease as though a spirit was trapped like a genie under my skin and would burst out furious if Lakis came nearer.

It was best to stick to the non-science-prone, I thought.

THE GENERAL WOULDN'T like science. I was sure of it. He loved poetry. He was like me. I wondered if he talked to himself. I wondered if his parents thought he was crazy when he was a child, just as mine did, and tried to stop it. I wondered if he liked trees. I wondered if he used to talk to trees the way I used to when I was little, though my parents thought it was myself I was talking to and said:

"Only little babies talk to themselves. Are you a blabbering idiot?"

"I'm not talking to myself. I'm talking to this tree."

"Ah."

They did not believe me. When they got to believing me, they took me to Dr. Andreades in Athens who had seen me since I was a baby and was the doctor for all my cousins.

"What's this I hear?" he asked. "You talk to trees?"

"Not *all* trees."

Some, like lemon and orange, apricot and almond, were not proper trees but more like bushes high above ground; they were like little girls their mothers dressed in organdy and ribbons and combed their hair in place, who looked at you shyly as if to say, "Am I not pretty?" and made you feel as shy as they. Others, like cypress trees and elms, kept their thoughts and feelings to themselves like someone proud and, if you spoke to them, would say, "What do *I* know?" But big, gnarled trees like plane trees and oaks and olive trees and fig trees and pines had seen and suffered a lot. They were severe but patient and kind. They were wise like the stylites,

I thought, the saints who stayed up on pillars and did not move for the glory of God.

Trees had their own personality. Trees were like us. Why did my parents think there was something wrong with me? It wasn't as though I talked to doors and stones. I *had* once talked to a rock but it wasn't a loose rock, it came out of the earth like a big wart and had great character. It was a live rock.

I explained all this to the doctor.

"Did the rock talk back?"

"Rocks don't talk." I laughed. "They listen."

"Do trees talk?"

"They have a silent language."

"Can you understand it?"

"Not when they talk to each other. When they talk to me, I do."

"What sort of things do they say?"

"They answer my questions. I tell them what I think and they tell me if it's dumb or funny."

"Do they speak with their leaves?"

"No. They speak with their body."

"Do you speak to them when you're with other children?"

"No."

"Why?"

I was silent.

"*Why?*"

"It wouldn't be polite."

"Anna! Is *that* the reason?"

"Other children think trees are for climbing," I said, upset. "All other children think trees are for climbing."

"You don't climb with them?"

"No."

"You've never climbed a tree?"

"I'm too frightened."

"*You* frightened? I thought you were fearless, Anna."

"I *am* fearless. But climbing is different."

"Maybe you haven't tried. You should pick out a tree and say, 'I'm going to climb this tree,' and see if you can't climb it. Okay?"

"Okay."

"Then you'll be like the other children. You'll play with them more. You'll talk with *them* more. Wouldn't you like to have friends?"

"Yes."

"See?"

"Okay."

One afternoon I went to the mulberry tree in the yard and said, "Mulberry Tree, I'm going to climb you."

The mulberry tree was the most beautiful tree in the garden, smooth-barked, lissome and full-leaved, still young and gentle, neither too forbidding, nor too dignified to climb. It was beautiful and tenderhearted, I thought.

Its trunk, soft and smooth to touch, was hard to grip. I slipped. I tried again and got up a ways, then slipped again. But I was determined to climb it and did climb it.

I got to the top, sat on a branch and thought, I've done it! But I felt none of the delight I had seen in other children. I was all sweaty. I shook from head to foot. I was petrified. If I move now, I thought, I'll fall. If I breathe deeply now, I'll fall. Ah-ah-ah, an intermittent, half-stifled grunt came from my throat. Ah-ah-ah!

Manolis walked by and looked up, astonished. He picked me up in his arms and set me down. My body was like a rag. Manolis looked at me and did not say a word. He went his way.

I'm not like other children even when I try, I thought. I envied them, envied their joy, how they climbed to the top and cried, "Look at me! Look at me! Look here!" and saw the world from up above, infinite and small and themselves like kings.

I was different, I thought. I lacked in something. And I was a coward. First and foremost, a coward.

Now I've laid myself bare.

A FEW WEEKS after I'd seen my first dead snake, Manolis and I were going to a shepherd's hut to buy a head of cheese, Manolis walking ahead, me trailing behind, when suddenly a snake crossed between us. It was no more than a yard long, fat and sluggish, snub-nosed, its eyes dulled and pained as though it was hurting. Maybe it has a stomachache, I thought.

Manolis realized I had stopped following him and turned around.

"I saw a snake."

"Where?"

I had never seen him so agitated.

He picked up a rock with his right hand and with his left he held me against his back. The snake had plodded along and disappeared, however.

We walked side by side for a while, Manolis breathing hard. I had imagined live snakes would be perky and mean, with steadfast venomous stares, that they would slither and sway, swishing their tails in disdain. I was surprised.

We got to the shepherd's hut. Manolis went in and I waited outside. A second snake crept by my feet, smaller and slimmer than the first, a lithe and lean, small creature that gave me a stealthy glance and glided away.

Live snakes! I thought. Finally.

"Hey, little snake," I said. "Where do you think you're going?"

I wanted to nudge it with my foot. My toes wiggled, tempted.

Manolis came out from the hut just then.

"Don't move!" he said.

He ran after the snake and crushed its head with his heel.

"Cussed critter!" he said.

He pulled up his pants by the waist and tightened his belt as though to see if he'd grown bigger the way men do after a fight.

"What did you say?" I asked.

"Nothing."

"You said cusscritter or something."

"I cursed it."

"Why?"

"It's Satan's thing."

"This snake here?"

"Don't you know from the Bible, girl?"

"That snake's been dead for a million years."

"Ten million."

"So?"

"That was the archsnake. This snake here comes from the archsnake. God threw out the archsnake same as he threw out Adam and Eve. He gave them all a kick. 'From now on, you crawl on your belly, creep,' He said."

"How did it crawl before?"

"I don't know how it crawled before."

"You shouldn't have killed it. I liked the little snake."

"Eve liked it, too, and sinned."

It couldn't have been the same type snake, I thought. If the little snake had said to me, "Eat that apple—it's good," I would have said, "Oh, go away. It's *my* apple."

The snake of paradise must have been bigger and old, I thought. Wrinkled. Very, very wrinkled with folds under its chin and bags under its eyes, no glimmering, gliding, tight-skinned thing that made your toes wiggle. That snake must have been hideous. Eve must have listened to it repulsed, horrified, the way one listens to people who have an evil eye and an evil tongue and say ugly things about others. Eve must have bit the apple already penitent. She must have loved the apple with all her heart and thought it good and beautiful for God had given it to her and said, "It's for you, Eve. Just for you. It's as beautiful as you, and I meant for you to have it." Eve held it on her palm, red, shiny, warm from the sun, and was happy.

God had given her the apple Himself. She hadn't plucked it as people thought. The Tree of Knowledge was no apple tree. The Tree of Knowledge bore no fruit. It was big and had branches that spread high and wide and had many leaves all the same size, that didn't flutter and didn't change color and didn't fall. It was magic.

The snake was envious, I thought, low-down, surly, hateful. An ugly, abominable creature that said, "Bite your apple, Eve, and see if it won't rot. See how good it *really* is. You think you've got something, woman. I tell you, you don't." Eve ate the apple in sorrow, in despair, the apple she had loved bitter on her tongue, sickening like blood sucked from a bleeding wound—the kiss that hurts and heals.

"What happened in Paradise wasn't Eve's fault," I said. "It was the snake."

"That's what I said."

"But it wasn't *this* kind of snake."

"This kind."

"How do you know?"

"I know."

He was being wrong-headed and mean and I was angry at him. If he tries to kill another snake, I'll bite his hand, I thought.

We started on our way home walking in silence, Manolis close by my side. The angrier I felt, the closer to me he walked. We fell in step, one-two one-two, stomping the ground.

"I don't like you."

Manolis was silent.

"I don't like you one bit."

Silence.

"You're a killer."

Silence.

"Killer! Killer!"

I stopped, Manolis stopped. I started, Manolis started. Finally I stood still in one spot and refused to budge.

"I have to make taps," he said.

"Go on."

"You can't stay in the woods alone."

"Says who?"

"Says I. Walk."

"I want to see if more snakes come out."

"No more snakes will come out."

"Why?"

"There're things that got no becauses. Who asks questions gets warts."

"What kind of warts?"

"On the hands."

"You get those when a frog pees on you."

"On the backside."

"You get those when you count the stars."

"Yeah," he said. "And when you ask questions."

I never looked up on starlit nights. I had no desire or interest to count the stars but I was afraid I might inadvertently anyhow, the way I stepped on sidewalk cracks even as I tried to waddle from side to side to place my feet dead center.

"What kind of questions?"

"Walk and I'll tell you."

I walked.

"God likes to have secrets," he said.

"What are His secrets?"

"How many stars has the sky. How many pebbles has the sea. How many hairs has your head—"

"*My* head?"

"Everybody's. How many grains in the sand. How many—"

"God's secrets are all numbers?"

"Numbers and other things. If you try to find out, He makes you insane."

He took the head of cheese out of the sack and kissed it all over. "Insane," he said. "I-n-s-a-n-e!"

He put the cheese on his head.

"I'm the king of France," he said. "On your knees. Kiss my feet."

We were by then out on a clearing, by the public road. I kneeled in front of him. As I bent forward my barrette broke and my hair came loose covering my whole body and the ground around Manolis' feet.

"Get up! Get up!" he said in a changed voice. He put the cheese back in the sack, held it under his left arm like a football and stood at attention looking over my head. I turned around swiveling on my knees. A military jeep was coming in the distance. It slowed down when it spotted us and came to a halt.

I stood up and shook my head back to get the hair away from my face. It was the general!

Manolis saluted.

"General, sir!" I stammered.

"Lady vamp! Come, let me give you a ride."

"In the front with you?"

"In the front with me."

I got in the car and the general set me on his knees. Mano-lis stood at the edge of the road, his shadow long and lone-some on the grass, his face sullen, saluting till the car got out of sight. The sun had begun to set and the woods were dark behind him. He'd have to go the rest of the way on foot, alone.

"Come on," said the general. "You're with us now. Don't look back. . . . This is Sotiris," he introduced the driver to me.

"Hi, Sotiri."

"Shall we order him to burn rubber?"

"Let's."

"Sotiri, on the assault!"

Sotiris pressed on the accelerator and the jeep jolted for-ward jostling us from side to side and throwing us up and down. The general laughed and held me tightly in his arms.

"I bit my tongue," he said. "Ouch! No good to laugh when Sotiris is driving."

We were on a road that had been heavily landmined and was still "provisionally" filled with rubble. The landscape was scorched and gutted.

"Ah, child, child . . ." he said. "You aren't having fun." He turned to Sotiris. "All right," he said. "Enough."

Sotiris looked at him out of the corner of his eye with impertinence, I thought, as if to say, "You sure now?"

The general looked down.

We had come to the road that went uphill and led to the barracks.

"The beret more straight," the general said to Sotiris. "You look like an artist."

"I *am* an artist," Sotiris said, tossing his head back. He did nothing about the hat.

The general reached to straighten it for him, his hand

going gently to the back of the soldier's head and staying a
long moment there.

"Yes, you are," he said. There was irony and sadness in his
voice.

Sotiris looked straight ahead, driving at an even, slow
speed, as though at the head of a long convoy. I moved to the
edge of the general's knees and held on to the dashboard.
Something had happened that had suddenly changed his
mood and I felt him behind me becoming stiff and cold.

We could now see the barracks, depots of corrugated metal,
low, long, identical buildings without roof tiles, dirt roads
marked with whitewashed stones on the sides like margins, a
few trees looking stunted, desolate, out of place. The Greek
flag, the cross symbol of the martyrdom and faith of our
nation, blue as our seas and skies, white as the ancient marbles, snapped in the wind like a door in a deserted house slam-
ming shut and opening again, a sound protesting emptiness.

Sotiris stopped in front of headquarters, a two-storied
building with a terrace on the second floor. No shutters, no
roof tiles, a simple rectangle.

The general let me out first, then went on ahead. He did
not say good-bye to me, he did not say "come along." What
do I do now? I thought. There was so much I had wanted to
tell him! The car ride had been short, awkward and uncom-
fortable, and I had not said a word.

A group of officers came out of the building. They saluted
and stood at attention till the general got to the landing,
then made way for him to pass and followed behind him.

"General!" I called after him.

They all turned around. The general looked surprised.

"Thank you for the ride," I said.

The general smiled.

"And, and—"

The officers stood around us in a semicircle.

"I saw a live one."

"A live what?"

"A live snake."

"Very interesting."

He turned to go.

"And, and—"

The officers looked at me with amusement.

"I liked it. I wanted to tell you I liked it. I saw two really. A big one and a small one. I only liked the small one. It was like this—"

I showed the length with my hands.

The officers burst out laughing. It was a mean, mocking laugh. The general looked away from them and did not even smile. Tears flooded my eyes.

"Anna," he said quietly. "Child, it's my fault. I'm sorry."

He put his arms around me, then pushed back.

"I must go," he said. "Good-bye, dear."

What did he mean, "it's my fault"? What was his fault? Why had the officers laughed at me?

I went by my father's office.

"What's wrong?" he said.

"Nothing."

He went on with his paperwork.

It was five kilometers from the barracks to the house and I did most of it running. I arrived at home in a sweat, out of breath, my hair wild.

"You have too much hair to wear it down," my mother said. "You look like a trollop."

A LONG TIME passed. I had seen every variety of snake there was—some two and three times—and Manolis had stopped bringing me more. My education concerning snakes was complete, I thought.

During that summer I went with Manolis to Mr. Papapolitis' farm to get fruit and vegetables. Mr. Papapolitis had a cistern with lilac bushes and pots of geraniums around it, and I liked to sit on its ledge and look at the still, greenish water. There were frogs in it, and insects boating on leaves, and big dragonflies that swooped down for a swim and came up again splattering drops of water. It was beautiful and cool, and I liked to wait there.

"Don't fall in," Manolis said to me each time.

And I said, "I won't. And if I do, I know how to swim."

"Swimmers have drowned."

"Not good swimmers."

"Good swimmers."

He walked to the farmer's house looking backward, calling, "If you drown I'll kill you!"

One day, parting the lilac branches to get through, I saw on the cistern ledge a giant slug, purple-black in color, smooth-skinned and slimy. It was sunning itself, disgusting and unperturbed.

"Manoli!" I screamed. "Quick!"

Manolis ran back. He saw the slug and, still out of breath, shrugged. "God's snake," he said.

"It's a snake?"

He nodded.

"God's! How come God's?"

" 'Cause it's His."

"God has a snake? Why?"

"It so pleases Him."

"*Pleases* Him? It's disgusting."

"Pleases Him."

"Kill it!"

Manolis wouldn't kill it. It was a sin to kill God's snake, he said, because it was God's gift to people He liked, a sign of His love and a blessing. When it came into your house, you were supposed to keep it and give it milk to drink and not disturb it but let it sit where it wanted and live with it.

I was appalled. That wasn't how God revealed Himself! As far as I knew, He spoke from fiery bushes, through the mouths of angels and, at His strangest, the beak of doves.

When our religion teacher first told us of the Baptism, I thought that as John was about to plunge Jesus in the River Jordan, a pigeon had waddled up to him going *coo coo,* the way pigeons do, which John understood to mean "This is My only Son in Whom I am pleased." My misapprehension was corrected when the teacher showed us a picture of Christ ankle-deep in water. Over his head was a dove, spreadeagled like a prefiguration of the cross and surrounded by golden light—no ordinary pigeon that jerked its head back and forth as it walked and went *coo coo* as though having a rumbling stomach. Still, quite clearly: a beaked bird.

"Did the dove speak in pigeon or in Greek?" I asked the teacher.

"In Hebrew."

"In Hebrew! But then, didn't the Jews hear and believe?"

"Those who have ears can hear."

"Didn't the Jews have ears?"

"They still don't."

The notion of an earless, faithless people was too harrowing. It can't be true, I thought.

I asked my mother when I got home, "Do Jews have ears?"

"Certainly they have ears. They are people like us."

"I know they are people like us. I thought maybe they didn't have ears."

"Mr. Simon is a Jew," she said.

Mr. Simon was the cobbler, a short, white-haired man with thick glasses and bushy brows. He looked at his own shoes when he walked and other people's when he worked, his eyes always cast down, his shoulders stooped. When someone said good morning to him, he said, "Good morning and good evening for later. And merry Christmas when it comes. And a lucky new year. And a happy name day, too," and then told a joke or two, and no one could understand where he learned his jokes, a man who lived alone and worked all day in a small lean-to without a window and a kerosene lamp that gave out fumes.

I spent long times at his shop for I liked to hear his hammer go tack tack, tack tack and see him keep the nails in his mouth between his teeth and take them out one by one to use them. He let me put nails in my mouth, too, and took them out one by one as he did his and nailed them to shoes saying, "What would I do without you, Annio? Want to be my apprentice?"

I ran to his shop at once.

"Are your ears real?" I asked him.

He looked up, surprised, then smiled and wiggled his left ear.

"Can *you* do that?" he said.

I could not.

The religion teacher talked nonsense, I thought. Nevertheless, I believed the Bible. I believed pictures. I believed people. I took them at their word. How could I doubt Manolis?

I looked at the snake with devout disgust. Soon it slipped down and crawled away.

"Is Mr. Papapolitis blessed then?" I asked Manolis.

"Yes, he is."

Mr. Papapolitis came toward us carrying a balance with fruit in the tray. From years of digging and weeding his back was bent permanently at the waist. His eyes were bloodshot and watery and he had a hoarse voice.

"Ach, little bones! Ach! Ach!" he said, rubbing his waist. "Why am I not a dead man?"

Maybe it's *Mrs.* Papapoliti who is blessed, I thought. I had never seen her. She raised hens and took the cows to pasture. It was her farm, too. Maybe God had sent His snake for her.

"How goes it, Mr. Papapoliti?" asked Manolis.

"Hard earth, hard life," said Mr. Papapolitis.

"It's been a good harvest," said Manolis.

"Good harvest, happy banks," said Mr. Papapolitis. He weighed the fruit and emptied them in our basket.

"Fruit today, shit tomorrow," he said.

"Ever so," said Manolis.

Mr. Papapolitis left, panting and groaning.

"Where did the snake go now?"

"For a walk."

"Will it come back?"

"Tomorrow."

ALL EVENING I paced up and down thinking about God.

"Stop swirling like a demon," said my mother. "You're driving me crazy."

"I'm thinking about God."

"She's thinking about God!"

She sighed.

"There *is* no God," said my father.

"Who made the world then?"

"It made itself."

"How?"

"How did *God* make it?" he said.

"Some people believe God made the world," my mother said. "Some people believe it made itself. There's no proof either way. You'll have to make up your own mind."

"Now?"

She laughed. "You have a long time—till you grow up."

"How old?"

I wanted to know, in one year? Two? Five?

"It's different with everyone. But when a person decides, they've grown up."

"What if I make up my mind now?"

"You can't now. You're too young. You must believe in God—children must believe in God."

"Children believe what they're told," said my father.

"Do *you* believe in God, Ma?"

"Yes, Anna," she said. "I believe in God."

KNEELING BEHIND THE geranium pots, hiding my face among the red flowers, I watched the snake on the cistern day after day, with shameful awe, enthralled and revolted. That's God's snake, I thought, *God's!*

What did I know about God? A long time ago, when I was four, I had seen Him in a dream.

"Hello, Annoula! I'm the good God," He said.

"Hi, Goddie dear. How are you?"

"I have an earache," He said.

That was all. I woke up. Poor God, I thought. He had looked like Father Gerasimos, Grandpa Damien's childhood friend who grew up to be a priest and visited at Grandpa's often. When he came the family sat in the great "sala," formal and attentive, Father Gerasimos in the place of honor. I was a nuisance, they said—clambering on his lap, pestering him to tell me stories, kissing him too much—and was banished from the sala when he was to come. But Father Gerasimos did not think me a nuisance, I knew. Father Gerasimos loved me. I waited behind the door till I heard him say, "But

where is *Anna?*" and then burst into the room crying, "Here
I am!" running to his knees and sitting on him astraddle.

Father Gerasimos' eyes were as though they'd never seen
or imagined evil—they never showed anger or surprise but
were always the same calm, kind love. His mouth was tender, serene, gentle in the wildness of his beard, like a soft
bright flower among coarse dry thistle. His lips were beautiful—they were like a wonder, I thought—but he didn't let
me kiss them. He said firmly, "no," each time I tried. I kissed
him everywhere else, however.

I told him he looked like God the day after my dream.

Father Gerasimos laughed.

"You do! You do! I've seen Him."

"Oh, well. If you've seen Him."

I took my little comb and said, "Be good and stand still.
Anna will now comb your beard."

My parents and Grandpa and my aunts—everyone in the
room—jumped out of their chairs to stop me.

"Let the child do as she wants," Father Gerasimos said.

"But Father—"

"No, no. Let her."

I combed his beard and said, "Beautiful priest, *ooo!* Beautiful!" and he caressed my hair and smiled. That's how God
would be with me, too, I thought.

That year, between ages four and five, my father was stationed in Athens and we lived in Grandpa Damien's house.
Grandpa was schoolmaster in a school for boys, a man of cir-
cumscribed experience and immense learning, weighed con-
victions and curtailed ambition, who was fair and righteous
but scoffed at kindness as undisciplined emotion. He taught
me reading, writing, arithmetic, the legends of Jason, Hercules and Theseus, the *Iliad* and the *Odyssey,* the stories of the
Gods, making me go to his study every afternoon and sit at a

small table, back upright, legs close together and straight, hands on the table with fingers entwined. No interruptions, no questions were allowed except when Grandpa paused and, tapping his ruler on his left hand, without looking at my stupefied face, said, "Anything you want to ask before I go on?" and went on shortly. If I fidgeted, he hit me on the top of the head.

"I don't love you, Grandpa Damien," I said.

"I'm not teaching you to love me. I'm teaching you to learn," he said.

I learned my first lessons about virtue and fortitude and honor. About dignity and pride. Heroism. Moderation.

"Who shames himself is not Greek," Grandpa Damien said.

Grandpa's was not the Christian ethic. His teaching did not aggrandize humility and charity or admit grace. There were no retributions, no punishments, no specters of Hell. Ostracism, total dishonor, was the threat used.

The rule was: "Don't do what will make you blush."

I, an easy blusher who blushed over my whole body and blushed to have blushed, thought life would be walking on pins and needles. I always blushed by surprise. I never knew *when* I'd blush.

"You'll know in time," Grandpa said to that.

He lectured pacing back and forth, striking the table with his ruler as he passed saying, "Wake up!" Then he'd interrogate:

"Who was Thetis?"

"Achilles' mother."

"Why did she put Achilles in the fire?"

"To make him immortal."

"How did she hold him?"

"By the heel of his right foot."

"What do you think happened because of that?"

"I don't know."

"Think! What had the Gods told Thetis about the fire?"

"Everywhere it touched the body, the baby would be immortal."

"So?"

I was silent.

"Did the fire touch the body everywhere or did it not?" he hollered. "I ask you. Answer me! *Answer!*"

"I don't know."

"Think!" he said. "Think!"

I thought but it did no good. How would I know? I hadn't been there. No one had been there. Thetis had not wanted anyone to see her. Grandpa said so.

"How did she hold him, I ask again?"

"By the heel."

Finally I got the implication.

"His heel was mortal."

"Right."

Nevertheless, the rest of Achilles would be immortal, I thought. Only his heel would rot.

If Grandpa Damien took it upon himself to make me a proper Greek, Father Gerasimos, inadvertently, made me a Christian. This big, beautiful, robust man with strong, willful hands and a face that showed a serene magnificence, looked as though he'd always known what he knew, always believed what he believed. He spoke and it was the truth and people believed him. Even my father revered Father Gerasimos—my father who thought priests were charlatans, hypocrites, sycophants, prostitutes of the spirit, in their chastity an insult to manhood and denigration of the sex of all men.

Father Gerasimos' way of teaching was as different from Grandpa's as was his doctrine. He started me with the Old Testament, telling me the stories in it as though they were fairy tales—the hero never truly harmed, triumphing in the end, vindicated fully. I thought the Old Testament was like the *Tales from the Brothers Grimm,* the *Arabian Nights,* the *Red Tied Yarn* and other books of tales my aunts read to put me to sleep or keep me quiet. Daniel, David, King Solomon and the Queen of Sheba became for me like Goldilocks and Aladdin and Puss-in-Boots, and the Hebrews' God like a big bad witch who was sometimes good.

Then we got to the story of Christ.

"This is the New Testament," Father Gerasimos said.

I didn't like the New Testament. The parables were tedious, I thought. The miracles were unexciting: bread-loaves and fish multiplying, sick people getting well and dead people reviving. The only miracle I liked was when Satan was driven into the swine and ran off a cliff crying, "My name is Legion!" The rest of the miracles were boring, I thought. Christ had a dull life and I didn't particularly want to hear about it. But when the end came—Christ's humiliation, torture and crucifixion, his despair and defeat on the Cross when his father abandoned him and Christ cried— my body tightened in Father Gerasimos' arms and I started sobbing.

"I don't want him to die—I don't."

"He came back to life in three days."

"I don't care if he came back to life. I don't want him to die."

"Don't cry, Anna. We'll go back to the part when he was a child."

He started to tell me the story of the life of Christ again, a little each day as he had the first time. But now it was different. Now I knew Christ would die in the end. Now, I listened with tears in my eyes and pity in my heart. Now, all Christ's deeds, all Christ's words had the import of a dying man's. His teachings were not like commands, I thought. They were last wishes.

It wasn't as with Grandpa's heroes when they died, when I marveled, not grieved, and felt myself bigger aspiring to their grandeur. Christ's death made me sad, humble, penitent for my pride.

I stopped climbing on Father Gerasimos' lap. I stopped kissing him on the face. I sat by his feet and held his hand.

Father Gerasimos told me the story of the life of Christ several times, then he didn't speak to me anymore, only smiled at me and let me sit by his feet.

"We don't speak any more, Papa-Gerasime."

"Silence is of God, child," he said. "God's love is silence."

I didn't mind we didn't speak. I felt happy. I like God's silence, I thought. It's nice.

"Ach, Giorgi," said Grandpa, calling Father Gerasimos by his lay name. "You're undoing my good work. Look at the girl."

Grandpa, like my father, was an unbeliever.

"Anna, come here. Come to Grandpa, child."

I got up and went to sit on the chair next to Grandpa.

"Back straight, back straight," he said. "Don't gape."

I corrected my posture and closed my mouth.

"Giorgi . . . Giorgi . . ." said Grandpa. "The time that's passed . . . The second generation. Look at it!"

Aunt Evaggelia, Aunt Despo, Aunt Maro, Aunt Ermioni and Father Gerasimos all looked at me. Elengo, her apron askew, hairpins slipping out of her hair like pins in silk, stood in the middle of the room with the coffee on a tray and stared at me sternly, too.

I wished my parents were in the room, wished they didn't go out and leave me alone so much. I wasn't "alone," they said. I was in a house full of relatives. Didn't I want Mama and Papa to have fun? Didn't I love them?

In the village houses we rented, unrepaired and unpainted since the war, covered with shell holes and cracks from

bombs, shabby, bare, like houses in resorts let by the day, my
mother played solitaire or wandered restlessly from room to
room hiding her face in her hands and crying, wilting in sad,
lonely splendor like an open rose for which there is no vase,
that is stuck in a tin can and drinks rusty water. In Grandpa's
house with its wood-paneled walls, dark carpets, billowing
curtains and dense amber light, rooms cluttered with furniture, pictures in ornate frames, leatherbound books locked in
glass-door cases, bronze and gypsum busts—everything
clean, well-ordered and austere—my mother was, in her fan-
ciful clothes and arrogant glamour, like a deposed queen
who hasn't been told she has no power. It didn't matter: she
shone in the world, she was admired, talked about. She *lived.*
We were in Athens!

That whole year she was loving, joyful, generous—spend-
thrift with emotion like an ebullient child.

When they came home, my father ushering my mother
into the room where we all sat as though showing off a prize,
his eyes gleaming with wine, she tossed her hat on the table
and dropped in a chair.

"I'm tired—*exhausted,*" she said. "What is the child doing
up?"

"She wanted to say good night," said Aunt Despo.

"Oh, Anna! You wanted to say good night to Mama? Oh,
sweet child! Come here, darling." She opened her arms wide.
"Come quick. Then to sleep."

"You shouldn't have let her stay up," said my father.

But he was too happy to make an issue of it.

He kissed me and, putting his arm around my mother's
waist, took her to their room, laughing, calling from the
staircase, "Good night to you all . . . Good night!"

My aunts hustled me to bed: Aunt Ermioni, who was seventeen and shared her room with me, pushing me ahead of
her, saying, "Come on, come on! I'm asleep already," Aunt

Evaggelia holding my mother's hat by the rim as though by the scruff of the neck—carrying it at a distance from her body—Aunt Despo and Aunt Maro bringing up the rear.

Grandpa's was a busy household with relatives and friends always visiting or staying, a distant cousin part-lodger and part-servant, a kitchen maid, Elengo, and an animal population of two enormous ungainly poodles—mother and daughter, Paula and Paulette—Mimi, a vicious angora cat, the parrot Anaxagoras who shrieked, "Now or never!" and "Do you want to change places, Pop?" a silent, morose canary and seven goldfish that had recently died when I added salt and blue ink to the water and was caught red-handed, my aunts gathering around the bowl frantic, looking at the fish as they turned purple and went *plop plop plop* to the bottom, crying, "What a child!"

My father was their only brother. There had been six sisters but two had married and now only four lived at home. They were so used to having sisters, they thought I was one, too. I was a big little sister like themselves, I thought.

They all had short cropped hair that emphasized the squareness of their faces and similarity of features: high cheekbones, a straight nose, narrow even lips, big almond-shaped eyes wide apart and slightly slanted. They had uncommonly long lashes that cast fluttering shadows on the underlids and made their eyes look half-closed.

They were intelligent, good-natured women who wore simple clothes—mostly straight skirts and loose sweaters—who looked men in the face and were imperious, impatient, with them. They went to the university and wanted to have careers. Grandpa Damien was proud of them.

"Women have good, able minds. Loftier than men's. It all goes away when they marry—alas," he said. "Marriage can make a man wise." He chuckled. "Look at Socratis! But it turns women's mind to mush."

Nevertheless, he loved best his two married daughters who had let their hair grow and used makeup and dressed to please their husbands. And he was sweet on my mother, looking at her spellbound and saying her name as though it filled him with wonder: "Aimilia. . . ."

FATHER Gerasimos stopped coming to Grandpa's house. Weeks passed, the whole summer. He's been taken ill, I was told. He's in the hospital.

I watched Grandpa, my parents, my aunts go visit him and come back, as though from behind a curtain. They did not talk to me about him and when I asked they said, cutting me short, "He's ill."

"Very ill?"

"Yes."

One day Grandpa said he'd take me to see him.

My mother said: "You think you should, Father?"

"I think I must. She loved him. He asked to see her."

"But," she said. *"Because* she loved him. I think—I—" She stood as though to stand up for me but faltered. "She's only a child," she said finally.

"Children are not spared death," Grandpa said. "No reason they should be spared its knowledge."

My mother lowered her head.

Grandpa took my hand and, as I hesitated and dragged my steps, looking at my mother for help, he pulled me forcefully out of the house. I tugged after him, frightened.

In the cab, through the hospital park, up the steps of the big building stolid and unembellished like an embankment, a white fortress of death that life stalked outside, Grandpa did not let go of my hand but tightened the grip, his bony dry-skinned fingers pressing my small soft hand till it hurt and grew numb.

There was a large hall and then a corridor. We turned left then right till we came to some stairs. We went up them, got to a new corridor, turned left, right, and left again. How will we be able to find our way back? I thought. The corridors all looked the same. The doors all looked the same. The walls were green, a dull oil paint that looked moist as though the plaster was sweating, as though the walls were sick, breathing out sickness. The infested air seeped into my skin.

Father Gerasimos was in the ward, third class, a big long room with cots in rows. The window panes were painted white to keep the glare out and let light in. There were small white night tables and wooden chairs at the sides of the beds and directly over them, evenly spaced like exclamation points dangling in the air, naked lightbulbs at the end of long, black cords. They were on, marking the institutional time for "day," shedding muted shadows on the floor and walls, making the visitors' faces yellow, hollow under the eyes.

The sick men lay supine, their bodies covered to the chin, the sickness eating at them under the sheets as though their heads alone fought for life.

There was silence. A frightening silence. I hid my face in Grandpa's sleeve.

He pushed me back.

"Try to show a cheerful face, child," he said. "Make Father Gerasimos glad."

I remembered how I used to run to him in Grandpa's sala and climb on his knees and kiss him while my aunts cried: "No, Anna . . . Don't . . . Easy . . . Enough. . . ."

I walked slowly now, afraid to go near him.

He had grown thin. He wasn't a big man anymore. Only his eyes and mouth were the same.

On his night table, put in a drinking glass, were four daisies, their bright green leaves coming out of the water vigorous and lush, the flowers drooping meekly.

I went to the edge of his bed and looked down at him.

"Don't cry, Annoula," he said. "Where I'm going, I'll always be with you."

"Will I be able to see you?"

"No, child. You'll feel my love in your heart. You won't need to see me. Remember how we stopped talking to each other?"

"Yes."

"Now we won't be seeing each other. It's the same thing. When people love each other—when their love is God's— they don't need to be near. All you'll have to do is remember me and I'll be there."

"My love is mine. I love you with *my* love, Papa-Gerasime—with *all* my love."

"Your love is God's, Anna. True love is God's."

"Mine isn't I tell you. *I* love you—*I*!"

"Giorgi," Grandpa said. "Giorgi, my brother. You're tired out. Don't talk."

"We can only love God, Anna," Father Gerasimos said, "and love men with God's love, in God's name."

"I don't love God."

"You'll love Him when you have the understanding."

Grandpa pulled his chair closer to the bed and took me in his lap.

"The daisies have wilted. . . . Wildflowers don't last," he said. And then, as though talking to himself, his chest heaving behind me, sobbing, "The daisies in the field . . . ," he whispered, "where we used to . . . when we were youths . . . where we used to . . ."

Tears filled Father Gerasimos' eyes.

"Forgive me, Giorgi," Grandpa said. "Forgive me."

Father Gerasimos closed his eyes. Grandpa and I watched him sleep till the end of the visiting hour, a man dying poor, alone—a ravaged body in white sheets, on a narrow bed, under a naked light—a man loving God.

EVERY DAY I went to Mr. Papapolitis' farm and looked at God's snake. So, you are God's, I thought. So, you are God's . . .

One day the snake was gone.

"Mr. Papapoliti, did you let the snake out this morning?"

Mr. Papapolitis laughed. "Did I let it out?" he said in his hoarse, raspy voice. "It's not me who lets it out, child."

"It's not here."

"I reckon it's gone."

"Where to?"

"God knows."

When I lay in bed that night and tried to sleep, a horrid thought came to me: What if I was good and God loved me and I didn't know it? What if God sent His snake to me? What if the snake was in my room—*now*?

"Oh no, God dear," I said. "No!"

But there the snake was, coiled on top of the armoire opposite my bed, its head thrust out like a person's resting his chin on an open palm, looking at me as though to decide if I was indeed good.

I'm not, I wished I could tell it. But could I contradict God? How could I contradict God?

I watched the snake. The snake watched back. I didn't move. It didn't move. Neither one of us slept.

In the daylight I saw there was nothing more on top of the armoire than the battered suitcase and gray hatbox that had always been there. It must have been a shadow, I thought. There were always flitting, frightening shadows in my room at night.

The next night the fear came back. The snake was on the

armoire. I was certain—I could see it. It didn't matter that
in daylight I knew there was nothing there. It was there at
night—it came at night. I stayed awake terrified, watching.

Dark circles grew under my eyes, my face got thin and
pale, my body weak, light, queasy, as though the skin I could
touch and feel as my own covered a stranger's insides. I felt as
though seasick—my soul wrenched from, loathing, my body.
My mind could think as it always could think, my mind was
the same, but when I touched my heart, my hand dropped
down listless. I couldn't say, "This is me." It was as when my
front teeth fell out and I saw in the mirror my gummy grin
and pulled back disgusted. Who *is* this? I thought.

"You'll get new, beautiful, strong teeth," my mother said.

I doubted it.

When they did come out, they were rough-textured and
ridged like saws. They were ugly and big.

"I don't like them," I said.

"We can't send them back," said Manolis.

I pulled my lips apart with my fingers.

"Do you like them?"

"They're good teeth."

"Do you *like* them?"

"I like them."

Every day, for a long time, I showed Manolis my teeth.

"They're great teeth," he said.

Still, I didn't like them. I didn't like the way they grew
out of my body as though they sprouted. What if other
things started growing out? I thought.

Nothing happened for a couple of years. Now, a coarse,
squiggly hair had appeared under my arm.

"Ma!"

"It's a hair."

"I know it's a hair. Why did it grow?"

"Because it must."

It *must*?

"You're growing up, Anna," my mother said.

She explained I would get more hairs like that one. She explained where.

"And your breasts will grow and be like mine."

I was going to get *breasts*? What for?

She showed me how the skin around my nipples was beginning to puff up.

"It will hurt for a while," she said.

Of course it would hurt, I thought. Imagine big strange things like fists trying to push through!

It must be that my soul is changing, too, I thought. My body is changing and my soul is changing. How will it change? What's going to happen to my soul? I was horrified. I didn't want my soul to change. I liked my soul.

I wished I could pray to God not to change my soul but I couldn't. I couldn't pray to God anymore—not with His snake in my room every night. I didn't *trust* God anymore.

By winter I was emaciated. My gestures had become graceless, abrupt. I walked rigidly, self-conscious, sat away from others, withdrawn in myself, reticent. The shadows under my eyes had become deep hollows. Sometimes the muscles in my arms and legs twitched and I dropped things.

The army doctor came to examine me.

"Puberty coming too soon, too fast," he said.

He prescribed vitamins and naps. I needed, he said, to take naps.

But I couldn't take naps. When I was small, as far back as I could remember—when I was three and four—my father put me to bed after lunch and said, "Now sleep!" like a command. I wasn't tired enough to sleep. It was the time in the day I most wanted to run around and play.

"I can't, Daddy."

"You must."

He closed the shutters, then pointed his finger at me and said, "Shut your eyes and don't stir."

I lay on my back with my eyes closed trying not to stir, afraid to disobey him even in his absence, my mouth filling with saliva that over and over I had to swallow, till I thought I'd never stop and go through life *gulp gulp gulp* like a fish in a glass bowl that tries to scream but opens and closes its mouth in vain and its eyes pop out.

I stayed immobile for two hours every afternoon, every summer, till my father opened the door and said:

"Did you sleep?"

"No."

In the evening, he had me go to bed two hours early, taking me away from the other children who were still playing, saying so they could hear, "You haven't taken a nap—you can't stay out as late as the others."

I followed him inside miserable, humiliated, and cried into my sheets. The other children continued playing outside and I could hear their voices through my window. I wasn't sleepy at all—only unhappy.

When I grew up and started going to school, my father let me be. The unhappiest hours of my early childhood had now become the happiest. I took out my books and read, or wandered around the house daydreaming. There was no one to ask me why I wasn't doing something or what it was I was thinking. Everyone in the house, the town, all over Greece was asleep—I, the only one not sleeping. I was like the prince in "Sleeping Beauty," I thought. Life was enchanted. Now they wanted to take it away from me—those few happy afternoon hours when I was alone, all alone, quiet, unseen in the bright sunlight. My father said, "Sleep! You *must* sleep!"

I couldn't—I wouldn't. I was no longer the pitiful little kid who lay down still. I was grown up now.

AT CHRISTMASTIME MY mother had to stay at home and mind my little sister, who had the measles. I went to the children's party at the officers' club by myself.

The party was ceremonial—ordered, formal—the children in clothes that looked as though they had been borrowed from rich relations, shoes that hadn't been broken in, hair brushed back sleek and tidy, faces scrubbed clean. They stood stiffly, their expressions weary and apprehensive as though waiting to pass inspection. The parents were sitting in clusters of chairs pushed against the walls. On the end of a long table a pine branch had been set. On the other end, the presents—books wrapped in the same gift paper and ribbons in one-fold bows—were stacked in a pyramid. Between the gifts and the tree stood a paper manger with pop-out windows with numbers outside and pictures of toys inside.

After we were given our books, didactic editions of fables, we picked a number from a bag and, dutifully, one by one went to the manger and opened our window.

"A trumpet!" "A train!" "A dollhouse!" "A sack of gold!" The word was passed from child to child in excited whispers.

Mine was a box.

"A box!" "A *box?*" "A box . . ."

"Anna got a box."

"A box of what?"

"A box of nothing."

"Just a box."

And, as though it wasn't all nothing, just pictures on a piece of paper, they started to heckle me and catcall: "Ann-a got a bo-ox . . . Ann-a got a bo-ox. . . ."

The more upset I became the harder and more heartlessly
they teased me. They had started to serve tea and sweets but
I couldn't eat anything. I was afraid I would choke and cry. I
thought of General Dimitriadis. He was the only person in
the whole world who was kind to me, it seemed. He was the
only person who could understand me.

As if I had no more hope in myself, as if it wasn't the
unthinkable—barging unsummoned into a general's room—
I ran upstairs, my face burning, my heart pounding fiercely,
and stood in front of his door. I didn't even know if he'd be
there. I dreaded he would be. I dreaded he would not.

I knocked.

"Enter!"

He was sitting at his desk with his back to the door and
hadn't turned around.

"General, sir!"

"Anna! Is something wrong? You look sick."

I shook my head.

"General Dimitriadi, do you believe in God?"

"Do I believe in God?" He laughed. "Do *I* believe in *God!*
You've come to ask me if I believe in God?"

He is laughing at me, too, I thought. I couldn't hold my
tears back any longer.

"Anna! What *is* the matter, child?"

He made me sit down on his bed and sat down next to me.

"Have you just come from the party?"

"Yes."

"What did you get in the manger?"

"The box." I cried harder.

"The box! How nice!"

I shook my head.

"What do you think is in it?"

"I don't know."

"What would you like to be in it?"

"I don't know."

"Think about it. Whatever it is you'd like, that's what's in there. The box is the best gift of all. A trumpet is a trumpet and a doll is a doll. A box is anything you want."

"The children made fun of me."

"They're jealous."

I dried my eyes.

There was a knock on the door. "Aha! My tea," he said. "I thought you were my tea before."

An orderly came in and set down the tray on the general's desk. The general asked for an extra cup. The orderly left and came back with another teacup.

"Good," said General Dimitriadis. "We're going to have tea, you and I."

"Milk?"—"Milk."

"Lots of sugar?"—"Lots of sugar."

"Big piece of cake?"—"Big."

"Oh good!" he said. "Me too."

"General Dimitriadi, have you ever seen God's snake?"

"I haven't had the honor."

"Do you *know* of it?"

"No. . . . What is this God's snake?"

I described it.

"That!" he said. "What makes you think it's God's?"

I told him what Manolis had told me. The general became grave.

"All snakes are God's, Anna," he said. "God made them sly, God made them wise. God made them dangerous, God made them gentle."

"What about the devil?"

"What about him?"

"*His* snake. The snake of Paradise. How is it different from God's snakes?"

"It's not."

"Was it a big snake or a small snake, do you think?"

"Medium," he said hesitantly.

"About a yard and a half?"

"About."

That sounded right. "Was it old?"

"Yes, it was old."

"What I thought! What I thought *exactly!*" I was excited. I *knew* I couldn't have imagined it wrong. "Very, *very* old?"

"As old as the devil."

"Is the devil older than God?"

"Same age."

"Like twins?"

"More like the same person. If they were twins, they'd have to have a father."

"And a mother!" I said.

"Of course."

I'd always wondered who made the devil. But how could God and the devil be the same person?

"I shouldn't have said 'person,' " the general said. "God is not a person or 'like' a person."

"What is He like?"

"He's not like anything."

"He exists though?"

"He exists but we can't know Him."

I thought about all this.

"How can we believe in something we can't know?" I asked.

"We can believe in ourselves," he said. "If you trust what's good in you, what *feels* good in you, if you try to do your best, always your best—that's like believing in God. It *is* believing in God."

"But God won't help us?"

"No. God won't help us."

"And when we're frightened?"

"When we're frightened . . ." he said. "When we're frightened, we must say, 'I'm frightened.' Fear makes us know ourselves. It makes us stronger. It's as shameful to deny fear as it is to run away from danger. We'd be cowards."

"It's bold to be frightened?"

"Courageous."

I put my arms around him, hid my face in his tunic and cried.

"I love you, General Dimitriadi," I told him as I sobbed. "I love you!"

"Why, Anna!" he said. "I love you, too."

Suddenly his breathing changed. He pulled me closer to him and held me tightly against his body. It scared me the way he held me. I pulled away. The general's face was like a stranger's. It was a frightening face. An ugly face. Revolting.

I backed away with small, slow steps till my back hit the door.

The general's face became beautiful again. Sad, gentle. It's not his true face, I thought. He has that other face. He's always had that other face.

Did I still love him?

A Crow

MY FATHER FOUND a frozen crow and brought it home and showed it to us saying, "I found it in the snow. It died from the cold. That's how cold it is out." We all looked at it, sad and silent, thinking, poor crow, and left it on the floor till morning. The crow thawed and came to life during the night, and I woke up hearing the beating of wings, seeing a dark shape flying in my room, crashing on the floor like a toy that suddenly unwinds, then flying again, distraught, knocking against the walls like a person his head saying, "Oh, oh, oh! Why was I born?" It was not the bird but its ghost, I thought.

I ran to my parents' room and flung the door open, bursting in without stopping to knock. Encountering the supernatural was an exceptional circumstance.

"Daddy!" I screamed. "Daddy!"

It was only a few years after the war. My father's nerves were still taut, his instinct honed to kill. He crouched on the bed with a violent jerk as though he had been ambushed and said, panting, "What? What? What?" He was terrified.

As when I saw my mother crying and felt guilty, a sense, that is, of utter worthlessness, a feeling I would, and deserved to, be punished though I had done no wrong—the inadvertent witnessing of her sorrow sinful, I thought, as glimpses of her naked—so I felt now seeing my father frightened.

My mother staggered on her elbow behind him and said, "Anna?" but he pushed her down and sat up on the bed blocking her view. He had gotten a hold of himself and was now in a rage to have been woken up. He pressed his hands

on his knees and stared at me as though he hated that I was
his daughter.

My army upbringing did not admit emergencies or allow
an urgent manner. As flames leap behind him, a soldier
doesn't scream, "Fire! Fire," but standing at attention says,
"I report a conflagration, sir," and salutes his commanding
officer. In this the army was like the church—ceremonious,
unbending, using words you can't scream out or mean what
you say in them. To God I always spoke in plain Greek and
only said *Our-Father-who-art-in-Heaven* and *holy-is-God-holy-
almighty-holy-immortal-a-men* to be on the safe side and make
sure I had His attention. It was like whistling a signal. *Then* I
prayed. But my father did not tolerate breaches of decorum.

"The crow . . . the crow . . . is flying," I said.

"Did you knock before coming in?" my father said.

"The crow . . . the crow . . . I thought—"

"Don't mutter and look at me in the eyes when you
speak."

"The crow—"

"Forget the crow. Did you knock?" he shouted.

I said I had not.

"Go knock."

I went and knocked and came back to stand where I stood
before.

"What do you want?"

"There's a crow-ghost flying in my room."

"Go back to sleep."

"But there's a *crow-ghost flying* in my room!"

"To sleep!"

"Daddy . . ."

"There are no crow-ghosts. There's nothing flying in your
room. I'll hear no more nonsense. Go!"

I tried to protest and he said again, "There's *nothing* flying
in your room."

I went back and he was right—there was nothing.

It wasn't so dark anymore and the things in my room stood clear in outline, the first dawn light falling on them like a gray haze, making them look soft-contoured, remote like things in old discolored photographs, and it was as though I was looking at them from far away, from another time. Everything seemed gloomy as in a room that's been empty a long time, without life, without light. Except this was *my* room—I lived in it.

Gray light is dreary, I thought. I wanted to be a poet and write beautiful words about beautiful things but it didn't come out that way. "Night's black like velvet caressed my soul . . . ," a poet I loved said. Dawn's gray was like felt, I thought. How could I write a poem saying that? Yet it was true—I knew: I had a felt hat I didn't like. Cousin Mary had a felt coat with brass buttons she wore year after year, Aunt Vasilia always giving advice, saying every fall, "Buy felt. It's durable. Look at Mary." Mary was called "Durable" for that. She was older than all my cousins, dull and disliked. She had a penetrating glance and looked at you intently as though she knew things about you you did not, and grown-ups thought her wise.

I closed my eyes and felt a little better. Maybe the crow was a dream, I thought. When I get up, I'll write Cousin Mary a letter.

When we left Athens, Mary had put her hands on my shoulders and had said, "We'll correspond, you and I." Her letters related what she ate and read. I answered telling her what *I* ate and read. She went into considerable detail but my own letters were concise: "Dear Mary—We had stew, baked fish, *imam baildi,* stuffed grape leaves and spaghetti this week. I read *Robinson Crusoe.* I liked it so so. I kiss you—Anna."

I'll write her of the crow, I thought. Mary loves ghosts. I

started the letter in my head. "Dear Mary—We had a lot of chicken this week because Maritsa had the stomach flu. We also had rice with yogurt and boiled beef. I read *The Little Princess.* It made me cry a lot. I saw a ghost!! It was the ghost of a black crow . . ."

Maybe I did just dream it, I thought. But I couldn't have! I had dreamt of Grandma. She was knitting something. "I'm making you a ribillon," she said. There was no word "ribillon." I couldn't be making up such a word *now.* My grandma said it and I dreamt it. I went to my desk and wrote on a piece of paper *ribillon* in case I forgot, saying out loud as I scrawled, "R-i-b-i-l-l-o-n."

"Kakakakaaaa kakaaa" came like an answer.

I ran back to my bed and covered myself to the chin. Did ghosts talk? I remembered Hamlet's father from *The Illustrated Classics.* Yes, they did talk.

"Kakaka ka," the cawing continued. It was coming from behind the stove, from the corner.

I wondered if people who heard voices heard where they came from. I imagined if you heard voices it would be from some place over your head that moved as you moved, or from all around you, not some specific corner. That would be *really* crazy—to say: "I hear voices. They're coming from right there."

I'm hearing this with my own ears, I thought.

"I'm not crazy," I said aloud. "I hear cawing."

The cawing stopped as I spoke and restarted after a small pause. It was coming from nearer and nearer. The crow-ghost, denser than I had imagined a ghost would be, but very, very real, very, very there, stood on the floor by my bed, shifting from foot to foot as though dying to pee.

What does it want from me? I thought horrified. What have I ever done to a crow?

It looked at me for some time then flew to the window

and clutched the lace curtain with its claws, beating its wings in a frenzy, the curtain furling and unfurling around it—a black corpse twirling in white lace, saying *kaka kaka,* fixing me with beady eyes. It looked more indignant than unhappy as though death were a mortal insult.

It stayed entwined in the curtain for a while, then it broke loose and started flying, as it had at night, hitting its head against the walls. Then, suddenly, it shat, big yellow-green plopping globs falling all around me.

The crow is alive! I thought.

Shit was a sure sign of life. It was a *miracle* of life. I had always liked my own and looked at it and smelled it to make sure it was not something awful and strange that had come out of me but shit, real and mine, satisfactory. When I heard grown-ups say "shit" with disgust as though they wanted to spit on it, I thought, Maybe *their* shit *is* bad. *They* must be bad. I didn't trust them and I didn't like them.

The crow perched on the back of my desk chair. It flapped its wings and cawed fast, frantically, as though pressing a particular point, saying, "And *I'll* tell *you* this. . . . And *I'll* tell *you* this. . . ."

"Kakakak*aaa* kak*aaaaa!*"

"Crow, relax," I said. "Re-*lax!*"

It looked like a bachelor bird, I thought. Lonely and crotchety, solemn and edgy—like someone with a chip on their shoulder. I liked it, I decided. I would make a pet of it and tie a string to its foot and let it walk with me to school and back and have it fly like a kite as the sun set in the evening unwinding a long twine twisted on a little stick in my hand.

WHEN IT WAS time to get up, I put my clothes on and went out to wash my face. My father was in the hall putting his hat on. As I closed the door behind me the crow, who had been quiet for some time, started to caw again. My father and I could both hear it in the hall outside. My hand on the doorknob still, I looked at my father straightening his hat, our eyes meeting in the mirror.

"So, it wasn't dead," he said.

He pushed me aside, went into my room and opened the window. The crow flew out. The little paper that said *ribillon* spun in the wind and settled on his feet. He tossed it aside with his shoe and closed the window.

"I wanted to make a pet of it."

He looked down at the shit on the floor, then at me, and didn't say anything.

Manolis let himself into the house. My father and he saluted. My father left. Manolis came into my room to start a new fire in the stove. As he passed my bed, he slipped on the crow shit and fell.

"What *is* this?" he said. "Is it *bird*shit?"

"Of course, it's birdshit!"

I was offended. His doubt suggested it could be mine.

"So, it is," he said, amazed.

He fetched some newspapers and started cleaning it up.

"My father brought home a frozen crow last night. It defrosted and flew around and—"

Manolis wasn't interested in the explanation. Manolis did not like explanations. He said, "There are as many whys as becauses," as though that made both of them too plentiful to be of value.

He held up the little paper that said *ribillon.*

"Do you want this?" he said.

"Do you know what it means?"

"Rib-i-llon," he read out. "No."

"Do you think it may be a knitting stitch?"

"I don't know knitting stitches."

"Did you ever hear some woman in your village say she made ribillons?"

"No."

He brought the bucket and mop from the kitchen and started scrubbing the floor with soap and water, bent on his knees.

"Do all birds freeze in the snow?"

"No. Not unless they're sick—on their way to die."

"You think the crow was going to die?"

Manolis wrung the mop and nodded.

"You think it will lie in the snow and die again?"

He nodded.

"I'll try to find it and bury it," I said.

Manolis said nothing. He didn't seem to care one way or another that the crow would die. Birds made Manolis gentle and melancholic. Sometimes he looked at them with tears in his eyes as though they had nestled in his heart and come to life out of the love inside him, soft and bright-plumaged, fiery like cries of joy, sad like longing, proud, graceful, flying forever away leaving him empty.

But crows he didn't like. Manolis was particular and obstinate about his dislikes.

"Why don't you like crows? What's wrong with them?"

"They're crows," he said.

There was a young deacon in our church, a boy of fourteen whose voice had not yet changed. He was gawky and fidgety, ill-at-ease in the long habit skirt, his big torn shoes jutting out as though wayward and contrite, his hands knobby and strong, his face perky, nothing in his features suggesting a calling. He said "Kyrie" in a high squeaky voice and "eleison" in a harsh guttural voice without moving his lips, like a bashful ventriloquist blushing for his gift. The crow was a little like the deacon, I thought. Black-clad as though in service to God, grave and prim, its shrill, surly voice sounding severity and zeal. To be so ridiculously silly and put such a brave face on was valiant, I thought. A valiant crow! And now it was lying in the snow, a wing over its head, waiting to die, getting colder and colder till its heart froze.

I sat at the edge of my bed, elbows on the knees, my head in my hands. Manolis was gone. The floors were wet, scrubbed clean. In the corner next to the woodpile where my father had first laid down the crow—left like a death note, I thought, like bands of mourning—were three black feathers. I picked them up and put them under my T-shirt, next to my skin.

MY MOTHER HAD started on her breakfast, eating stooped over the table, my father's brown cardigan over an old house-dress of faded muddy-green wool with blotched crimson roses. It clung to her body loosely like a stocking that's taken the form of a foot. When she took it off, leaving it wearily here and there—a chair, the clotheshorse, a hook—it drooped empty, lonesome, like clothes of the dead, bereft. It had her smell, her sadness, her softness. I pressed it to my cheeks nights when she was out with my father dressed in finery— chiffon, velvet, shimmering silk, jewelry, lace—her beauty resplendent.

She pushed a cup of hot milk and a plate with cake down the table for me and turned to my sister Maritsa, who had been sleeping in my parents' room since she got the flu, and said, "Eat."

Maritsa sat on a chair pulled close to my mother's, holding her spoon upright on the table, gaping. She had pale skin, a delicate, graceful body, a small face with brown hair cut in bangs and straight across the sides and back, and big black round eyes. She followed my mother around the house

closely, her posture wavering, her gait tentative, timid—my
mother letting her trail after her, gentle, absentminded, talking to her without turning her head or looking down, Maritsa always being there.

My father believed you have to treat and train a child like
an animal till it reaches the age of reason, which he set
roughly at the end of the fourth year. He taught me when I
was an infant to stay away from the woodstove, saying, "It
burns! No!" taking my hand and burning it lightly. Not to
climb on chairs, saying, "You'll fall! No!" tilting the chair I
had climbed and making me fall. He taught me not to cry
when I was older, beating me when I did, saying, "Tears make
pain hurt worse."

When he tried this method on my sister, such was her terror, such the fear that stayed with her afterward—making
her whimper and crouch in corners when she saw him—that
he desisted.

He did not beat her, did not praise her, hardly talked to
her at all.

In the evenings when he came home from the barracks
and sat by the fire tired, he called her over, saying, "Maritsa,
come to my lap. Come sit here and make Father feel good.
Come, doll."

Maritsa went—reluctantly.

"Ach, cursed female nature," said my father. " 'No,' when
you're wanted."

But he smiled and looked at her with affection and was
tender.

MY MOTHER'S COUSIN Menelaos, who had been sent to a
farm to recover from whooping cough when he was four, an
anemic, spindle-limbed child, saw an ox pulling a plow,

plodding sadly as though in penance, a powerful animal humble before God, docile, patient. A farmer prodded it lovingly along saying, "Ho, beast! Ho!" Little Menelaos marveling, taken by the animal's stern melancholy, unwittingly branded himself "The Ox" for life, saying he wanted to be an ox himself. He grew to be tall and thin, an uncoordinated, gangly man with a big Adam's apple, protruding lips and blinking eyes, prematurely bald at twenty. This Menelaos, The Ox, on vacation from his university studies in England, stayed with us the summer before Maritsa was born and was the person to tell me of her coming. I was a little over three.

"Me Big Ox," he said.

I regarded him with suspicion. I had not seen Menelaos before.

"Big Ox love Little Pisspot. His heart go *thump thump.*"

He calls me "potty," I thought. Why, I couldn't imagine. I had a potty of white enamel like a huge cup. It had flowers in looped wreaths painted on it. Sometimes I put it on my head like a hat and went to my mother's room to visit. My mother laughed. I took it off, put it upside down on the floor and sat on it. My mother and I pretended to have tea.

"Big Ox give Little Pisspot kiss. *Moooch moooch,*" Menelaos said.

"What's an ox?"

"Ox big animal. Ox draw cart. Ox go *mmm mmm.* Ox strong. Menelaos when so small, he wanted be ox."

Uncle Menelaos wanted to be some kind of horse, I thought. I wanted to be a charwoman myself. My grandparents had a woman working for them dressed in black with a black kerchief around her face and neck. I watched her scrub the floor retreating with small steps to places that were still dry. She didn't talk to me. I wanted to work on my knees, too, and wear black and keep silent. I could not comprehend someone wanting to be an animal.

"Pisspot, you serious," The Ox said. "You grave. Sing a song."

"I don't know songs."

"Don't know songs! Ox teach you."

He taught me a song that he said was English and we held hands and jumped up and down singing it together over and over till my parents said to stop.

> I would, if I could
> If I couldn't, how could I?
> I couldn't, without I could, could I?
> Could you, without you could, could ye?
> Could ye? Could ye?
> Could you, without you could, could ye?

That was the song. English sounded like gibberish, I thought. It only had three sounds. The Ox was a peculiar uncle.

Menelaos' parents were in their late forties and had been married over twenty years when he was conceived, both of them small-boned, slight, with scant withered flesh, parsimonious and devout, always dressed in dark clothes and austere hats—unlikely parents of any child—formal in their affection, calling each other gently "my dear," hardly ever touching. When Aunt Roza began to show, the relatives said, "Good heavens! *Roza?*" It was unseemly. Uncle Kostis and Aunt Roza owned up to the fact—this protruding evidence of indecency in their old age—with embarrassment.

Menelaos was timid, prim, contorted with self-consciousness—crouching, dragging his body like an encumbrance, a mortifying burden, stooping his shoulders as though want-

ing to draw his head inside, ungainly slinking as he moved.
Coming in a room, lanky, disjointed, leading with his chin,
he moved his arms as though signaling people stranded forlorn across the shore. He said, "Hi! Hi! Hi, everybody," in a
piercing voice, sat on a chair pulled out for him and, stretching his legs, crossing and uncrossing them, he twitched his
mouth till someone began to speak. He did not converse.
If someone said, "I was up with the birds," or "I had some
great chocolate mousse the other day," or "When I travel I
always buy a new toothbrush," Menelaos interrupted saying,
"Birds—ha! ha! . . . Mousse—ha! ha! . . . Toothbrush—ha!
ha," repeating the last word and laughing while the speaker
looked at him stony-faced, perplexed, going on with his
story—an early rise, the delectable mousse, a newly pur-
chased toothbrush—only to have Menelaos interrupt again,
laughing with delight, saying, "Do go on! Do! This is super!"

"Anna's mama have baby in belly," he said to me.

I shook my head.

"Baby now small. Baby teensie-weensie. Baby grow big,
belly grow big. Anna see big belly. Anna believe Ox."

Mama can't have a baby in her belly, I thought. She
doesn't *eat* babies. And nothing can grow in the belly.

My father had assured me when I swallowed a cherry pit
no tree would grow in my stomach and come out my nose
and ears. He said, "Nothing can grow in the belly because
there's no light."

"Who put a baby in her belly?"

"Anna's papa put baby in."

"Where did Daddy find the baby?"

"Me boy, you girl," he said. "Me different."

"You have a birdie."

"Papa have birdie, too. Yes?"

"A *biiig* bird."

Menelaos laughed. "Papa's big bird magic," he said. "Papa

put big bird on mama's belly. Papa say, 'I want a baby to grow there.' "

My father's bird is a magic wand? I thought.

"How will the baby come out?"

"Mama go to hospital. Mama come back with baby. Anna play with baby. Anna happy."

"I don't want to play with a baby."

"Mama bring toys from hospital. Rattles . . . Balls . . . Little bunnies . . . Bears . . . Nice bassinet . . . Mama bring big black pram."

"Where's the toys now?"

"Toys in belly."

"The rattles and bears?"

Menelaos nodded.

"And the pram? Where is the pram?"

"Pram in mama's belly."

Nonsense! I thought. As if Mama's belly were a store. I was annoyed. He had been teasing me all along, I thought.

"What happened? What did you say to her?" said my mother coming in the room.

"I gave her the happy tidings."

"Oxxie! You shouldn't have! We wanted to wait a little longer. We should have told her ourselves first."

"Is it true all he said?"

"Yes, Anna. It's true," my mother said.

"See?" said Menelaos.

He tried to grab my skirt but I pulled away. I was angry he had told me what he did. It was his fault these awful things were to happen, I thought. If he hadn't told me, if I hadn't known, nothing would have happened. My father and mother would be the same as before. Now my mother was growing things in her belly and my father did weird hocus-pocus with his bird saying, "I want small babies put there . . . and little bunnies . . . and bassinets. . . ."

"Pisspot angry with Ox?" Menelaos said. "Pisspot don't like Ox no more?"

"Why on earth do you talk baby talk to her?" my mother said. "She has perfect diction. She's extraordinary for her age."

"Downright abnormal. You baby," he said to me. "You talk baby talk. You learn. Ox teach you."

My mother laughed.

I didn't look at them.

"Anna don't talk to Ox at all," Menelaos said. "Anna hard-hearted. Anna mean."

He was mean, I thought. *He* was hard-hearted. I tugged at my doll Oudi's arm, pulling him to a corner in the room, and sat away from them.

Oudi was as tall as I was. He had a porcelain face and the rest of him was pink stuffed cloth. When people saw him, they said, "Ugh!" Grandpa Damien called him albatross. Albatross was the name he made up for him, I thought, as I had made up the name Oudi. "Here comes Anna with her albatross," he said.

"I can't bear to see her dragging that thing," my mother said.

"Did it ever have clothes?"

"Tails and a top hat."

They laughed.

I sat looking at them talk but not listening, thinking, Daddy's bird is magical . . . Daddy's bird is magical . . . remembering how I put my arms around him all the time and pressed my face on his lap and touched my nose on his bird, crying, "Daddy! Daddy!" It didn't feel strange at all! It was just a thing my father had, I had thought, a part of his body like a dangling mole. How fooled I had been! I'd never, never go near it again. The thought of my father, all of my father, not just his genitals, filled me with unease.

When he came home, I didn't run to embrace him.

"Hi, Anna," he said.

"Hi."

I propped Oudi in front of me.

"How's my little daughter?"

"Well."

I'm not his little daughter, I thought. He's different from me. I am not his child. I have no magic powers.

MY MOTHER'S BELLY got big slowly. I didn't see it grow. Suddenly I looked at it and it was bigger and then again after some days, the same thing. It grew at night, I thought. My father lay on my mother when she was asleep and said with his bird what more he wanted the baby to have. He gave it everything but clothes. My mother knit those. I felt small hard lumps when I touched her belly—rattles maybe or a bunny's pointed nose. There wasn't anything soft. The baby must be way in the back, I thought.

Soon my father would add the pram and my mother would become enormous. I would be unable to see her face behind the belly. I wouldn't like that. The way it was now, I put my arms around it and it was as if I held all my mama in my hands. I loved my mama.

Sometimes something went *tap tap* inside her belly. It knocked against my cheek and I drew away. My mother smiled. "That was the baby," she said.

"Get away from there," the baby was saying, I thought. "This is *my* belly."

I was thrown. No, it isn't! I thought. It's my mother's— mine! I liked my mother's round belly terribly. I wanted it. I didn't think we would get along, the baby and I. I had a bad feeling about it.

When it was born they took me to the hospital to see it. Maritsa lay in a crib next to my mother's bed, screaming, her face red and blotchy. A bad nurse had doused her in scalding water, I thought. No, I was told. Babies look like that at first.

"Why is she screaming then?"

"Babies cry like that."

"Why is she screaming at *me?*"

"She doesn't know you, Anna," my mother said.

"Little sister, I'm big sister," I said.

With affronting, astounding insolence, Maritsa continued to holler *ouaaa ouaaaaa,* her face hideous with hate, her eyes squinting, her small hands in fists. I had never in my life been rebuffed so rudely.

I watched her with abhorrence. She drooled, I thought. She squealed. She babbled. She was uninterestingly—contemptibly—infantile. Nothing in her but wailing spite.

When the relatives came to our house and went to her crib saying, "Cute baby . . . sweet . . ." and picked her up and fondled her going gaga with affection and delight, I started to dislike *every*body.

"You must love Maritsa," my mother said.

Love was like food they forced you to eat saying it was good for you, I thought at four. I didn't like love. I refused to love. When my mother said I must love someone, it was always someone hateful. I didn't love anyone, I thought.

MARITSA, HERSELF NOW four, in my mother's arms, pale, weak, with bluish circles under her eyes, her head on my mother's breast, her small hand on her lap palm up as though in listless wonder, was being spoon-fed the last of her breakfast, swallowing with lack of interest, looking at Manolis as he cleaned the ashes in the stove.

The room we were in was the central hall of the house. The stove was against the wall opposite the front entrance

and radially around it at even intervals were the doors to the
other rooms. In the middle of the room stood a square folding table with four chairs where we had our meals and where
my mother and Maritsa were now sitting. Between the door
to the kitchen and the door to my parents' room was a military cot covered with a peasant red-and-white blanket and
three unmatched throw pillows. There were also some canvas
folding chairs and a big wooden trunk with metal hoops.
There was no carpet or pictures, but there was a mirror on
one of the walls in a tin corrugated frame with a painted gar-
land arched at the top that had come with the house and my
parents had not bothered to take down.

The entrance door opened to a small veranda with steps
leading to the garden. On either side of the door and adja-
cent to it were two large windows of undivided glass, uncur-
tained. I stood by one of them looking out at the snow.

There would be no school that day, as there had been no
school the day before, because of the weather. The snow was
about a meter deep, beginning to ice. No more was falling.
A strong wind made the icicles hanging from the tree
branches quiver. There was nobody outside. How slowly
time passed in winter, even though the days were short, I
thought.

I was about to move from the window and go to my room
and read, when my mother shouted, "Don't you *dare* go out!
You'll freeze," angrily as though she felt, "She'll freeze to
death and be trouble. I wish she *were* dead."

Without a coat, without gloves, I rushed out, stood on the
veranda in self-punishing, furious protest, tears freezing on
my cheeks, my hands and feet stinging with pain. I don't
like her either, I thought. I hate her.

In front of our house stretched a big field. A line of wil-
lows bordered its end, blocking the horizon abruptly like a
backdrop. They screened off the unknown, boundless world

beyond, their serene beauty disquieting. To the left were charred, sparsely wooded foothills landmined and burned during the war, behind them the stone mountain that rose over the village like a boulder, and to the right a cluster of refugee homes, long and squat, stunted, identical, carefully whitewashed, with clumps of grass in their parched yards and tufts of basil and sickly geraniums in tin cans by their doorsteps. They were now half-covered with snow, their rooftops as though adrift in a white flood. Starting at our house, going into the foothills through the field, were the trails my father and Manolis had made, each his own, without overstepping the prerogative of rank. They cut resolutely through the stillness, silence, infinite smoothness of the snow—parallel paths that did not converge, intransigent like duty.

Everything was an immaculate whiteness, without variation, without shadows, more frightening than darkness. In darkness you can't see and you imagine horrible things, I thought. Here I could see, see clearly, and saw nothing. I could *imagine* nothing. It was as though my mind was all emptied out. I felt an emptiness inside and outside me as though there was no life but mine in the whole world.

What did God mean by the snow? Sunshine was His joy and storms His anger, breeze His caress and wind His chastisement. What was snow?

What happens to all the animals? I thought. What happens to the birds' nests? How do the wild animals breathe when the snow buries their lairs?

My mother opened the window and said, "Get back in, tyrant . . . Tyrant of my soul, get back in," then closed the window to shelter herself from the wind and stood looking at me, her eyes behind the glass cold and damning, the look they had when they met my father's in the mirror the time she said, "Go around the boil," as he was shaving, her voice supercilious, peremptory. What he would have done as a matter of course now would be obeisance to her shrill command. He slid the razor sharply, firmly across the swollen flesh at his jaw's edge—blood and pus spurting in the air—and calmly continued to shave, his eyes looking at his reflection in the mirror dark with hate, whether for himself or her, I did not know. She looked at the pus with disgust then down at him like someone who has brought low a despised foe. She was incapable of direct violence but had an insidious, sadistic power to incite violence in him, a violence he turned against himself and often against all of us—one time almost getting us killed as we were driving in a small convertible, nearing a street of short steep steps that went five blocks downhill till it came to a wharf. My father slowed down to look at the view. My mother said, "Why did you slow down? You can't turn here!" My father turned. The car bounced down the steps, pouncing in momentary stops as it hit the intersections, continuing downward with increased momentum block after block. It flew over the wharf and came to a jolting halt inches from the water. He ordered us out of the car and raced away. My mother was calm. It wasn't the calmness of shock. It was the knowledge of victory, the vengeful vindication of her sanity over my father's madness. Holding Maritsa in her arms, myself following behind, she went back up the steps we had come down in the car. People were still hanging out their windows, crossing themselves in disbelief. Like a dignified actor in a play that is derided, she walked with her head up, defiant.

I felt the cold more and more. It did not feel like cold but like pain, a piercing, numbing hurt that brought more tears to my eyes. I couldn't lower my eyelids. My eyeballs are freezing, I thought. I stared wide-eyed, terrified, at the snow's bleak brightness.

"Anna," Manolis called. "Your father is on the wireless."

He held the military radio out the door.

"Get inside and *stay* inside," my father said.

I went back in.

"Are you crazy?" my mother said. "Are you insane? Are you mad? What are you, my God? What *are* you?"

Maritsa looked at me with wonder.

Manolis helped me take my shoes off. He took a basin, filled it with warm water and made me step in.

"Her nose will fall off," my mother said. "Her hands will get gangrene. Look at the way she looks! Look at her!"

Manolis rubbed my nose and then my hands, kneading at them slowly with worried patience. He was a farmer before the army and his hands had the gentle, firm grip—soft and sure—of a man's working the land, closing alike over manure and sprouting seeds, offending weed and blossom.

My mother stood by and watched, then went to her room and got her deck of cards. Sitting at the table, her body tense, her face apathetic, she laid them out and played solitaire—several games, each halfway through, not bothering to finish, muttering with equal disappointment, "It will come out," or "It won't come out," gathering the cards back in her hands, bitter, suspicious, as though being cheated by fate.

Maritsa sat on the floor playing with her stuffed monkey, setting it on its feet and letting go of it, saying, "Monkey, stand! Now, monkey . . ."

Slowly, feeling and then warmth came to my body.

"My skin itches."

I reached inside my sweater and scratched my chest. As I pulled my T-shirt, the three crow feathers fell out and dropped in the water. They floated, swirling around my feet.

"Mama, look! Feathers! There are feathers in Anna's foot-bath," Maritsa said.

My mother did not look.

"That should be enough," she said. "Anna, dry your feet."

I dried my feet in the towel Manolis held for me and went to my room to get my slippers. As I was coming out, Manolis was going outdoors with the basin. I ran to the window and saw him spill the water over the veranda rail onto the ground. It slid on the iced snow and almost immediately itself froze. The feathers stuck on the surface, small black spots in immense whiteness.

The Deer

MY FATHER SAID, holding the deer, "It knows no fear. Every newborn—animal or human—comes to the world in trust." He shook his head. "Trusting what?" he said. My father deprecated trust. Only fools trust, he believed.

He put the deer in my arms. It was wrapped in a towel like a foundling, its body a soft bundle of bones, warm and trembling. It's nervous and shy, I thought. Its heart beat fast and it nestled in my arms as though it wanted to hide. I felt love for it—immediately I felt love for it. A wonderful love filled my heart as though before it had been empty and now there was nothing in it but love.

"Do you want to bring it up?" my father said.

"What will happen when it grows up?"

"We'll keep it."

"A deer?"

He laughed.

"Mine?"

"Yours."

My father had given me a deer!

We took an army blanket down to the basement, put it in a corner bunched up, its folds deep soft furrows dark and dank like freshly plowed soil, and to the side we piled up logs of wood, dead tree limbs, moss drying on their bark.

I fed the deer with the bottle Manolis had been sent to buy in the village and cuddled it till it slept. My father, my mother, Maritsa and Manolis watched, then went upstairs.

The basement floor was unpaved and the cement walls moist with mould. A dim light from a small lightbulb by the stairs shed huge shadows and faded in darkness leading to the netherworld as the darkness of wells in fairy tales. Devils with ears on top of their head and tails, and imps, and magicians and witches and dragons lived there. Fairy tales are not true in themselves, I thought, but tell of true things nevertheless—things that can happen. How would I be frightened of the dark else? One can't be frightened of things that can't happen.

My mother called me for dinner and I went upstairs.

Manolis closed the trapdoor.

"What if the little deer wakes at night all alone?" I asked him.

"Its mother would have left it to go graze."

"She wouldn't go graze at night!"

"Makes no difference day or night."

After a while he said, "It's blind still. Babies are born blind. The blind can't tell day from night, can they now?"

When I was in bed, I thought, Are the blind frightened? It is as dark outside them as it is inside. They know the world through feeling, I thought. They know what's in their heart. The heart is gentle and kind. The heart is good. The heart is not fearful. The mind is fearful. It's the mind that frightens the heart. If we saw with the heart we would not be frightened. That's why babies trust—they are born blind. I'll explain it to Daddy.

I must have been born with my eyes open, however. I cried day and night, my father not letting my mother pick me up. He did not want my life to start in a lie, he said. We are not born to complain—we are not born to be comforted. Infants have no feelings, he believed. They only know hunger and discomfort. But I did have feelings, I thought. Infants do have feelings. Their wailing goes piercing like a knife through the heart and makes you stop your ears. The sound is pure anguish, pure dread. Aren't a baby's tears sor-

row? What is sorrow then? I had never seen sorrow on
grown-ups. Grown-ups grieved but held their grief inside
them as a miser his joy.

EVERY DAY I fed the deer and caressed it and talked to it and
told it stories. It can understand, though it cannot speak, I
thought. Its ears turned this way and that to the sound of my
voice and it lifted its head to my face and put its forelegs on
my chest and came close to my mouth to hear better. Its eyes
did not see for many days but its ears could see and recognized my steps and knew when I came near. One day—it was
quite sudden—its eyes became bright and clear, shining
with joy as though before it did not know what it was but
now knew itself to be a little deer, lovely and sprite and
sweet. I took it out in the garden and said to it, "This is the
world, little deer."

It blinked and twisted its ears. It looked startled. It's con-
fused, I thought. It looks as though its ears hear things its
eyes do not see. Its ears were alert and frightened, its eyes
trusting.

I sat under the apricot tree and the deer sat next to me.
When I got up, it got up, too. When I walked, it walked
close to me.

At night I put it back in its nest and left—as Manolis had
advised me—the door to the garden open. In the morning
the deer had gone out by itself. When I came down, it ran to
me and butted its head against my knee and bounced around
and made me run with it.

In a few weeks it was weaned and started eating grass. I
went to the meadow and cut branches for it and brought
them home and fed it from my hand.

My mother coming home one evening stopped in the garden and looked at the deer as I was feeding it and said:

"They *are* beautiful creatures."

She did not say "your deer," she did not say "this deer," she said "they."

Once when we were moving to a new outpost and had made a start before daybreak, we stopped for breakfast in a small village. The cafe had just opened and we sat at a table outside. The owner brought us warm fresh bread and honey and hot milk. There was no one in the streets yet. It was quiet. The sun was coming up and the air was cool and bright—clear as though the air *was* the light. It's so beautiful, I thought. My soul grew bigger and bigger—my soul filled my whole body and started to pour out of me. The more it poured out, the bigger it got. We got back in the car. I sat in the backseat crammed with the luggage and my soul became small again.

When something is beautiful, it makes the soul grow big as the world, I thought. Poppies are beautiful. And blooming almond trees. And peacock tails. And jewels. And the sky. And the sea. And dew in the morning. And wheat fields. When something is beautiful, you cannot imagine it any different or any better. Beauty is perfect as it is.

My deer was not perfect. His head was too small for its body, its ears too large for its head, its legs skinny and knobby. My soul did not grow big when I looked at the deer. My soul—all my soul—crept into my heart and made it jump and swell and flutter, and heart and soul then were one and my body got warm and happy and I thought, "I love my deer." Still, my deer's eyes were beautiful and its snout and its tongue and its ears and its rib-cage and its hooves and every little hair of its fur. My deer was the most beautiful thing in the world because I loved it.

Its beauty is a different kind of beauty, I thought. It's something more than beauty. My mother can't see it. My mother said "they." No one can see it. Only I can.

. . .

MARITSA WAS A little over four when my father brought home the deer. She didn't show any interest in it at first but when the deer grew and started playing in the garden and people stopped by the fence to look at it and guests went down to pet it and admire it, she became jealous and wanted the deer to be hers and, one day, threw herself on the floor and beat herself on it and cried, "Mine! Mine! The deer is mine!"

"It's mine," I said.

"Not yours! Mine," she screamed.

When my father came home she went to him and said:

"I want the deer to be mine."

"It's yours and Anna's," my father said.

"No! Mine! Mine alone," Maritsa said.

"Why should it be yours?"

"You give Anna everything."

"Anna is old and can take care of things. A small animal needs a lot of care."

"*I* can take care, I *can.*"

"All right then. It's yours."

"Daddy, you can't give it to her! It's mine," I protested.

"You can't say 'you can't' to your father, Anna. And what is yours is what I say is yours."

"But you did say it was mine. You gave it to me."

"I unsay it."

"She can't take care of the deer. You *know* she can't."

"Then she'll have to learn she can't. She'll have to learn one can't own what one can't handle."

"You're unfair."

"The matter is closed, Anna. The deer is Maritsa's. Maritsa will take care of it. If Maritsa can't take care of it, you'll have it back."

"I won't have it back."

My father was silent.

"I won't have it back. I don't care."

I went to my room, closed the door behind me and cried. He's unfair, I thought. He's not as I thought he was. He is unfair—unfair!

I did not go out in the garden the next morning. Manolis saw me stay in the house and looked surprised but did not say anything. Manolis does not ask questions.

Maritsa said: "The deer is mine. Daddy gave me the deer to be mine."

Manolis filled the tank over the kitchen sink with water from the well.

"It's mine," Maritsa said again.

Manolis picked up the garbage can and went to empty it outside.

"The deer is hungry," he said to me when he came back in the house.

"I don't care," I said. "Let Maritsa feed it."

Manolis asked permission to go to the fields and cut branches for the deer.

"I'll go, too," Maritsa said.

They went together hand in hand and I watched them return, Maritsa walking unsteadily, her feet swaying under the weight of the branch carried in her small arms.

She held the branch for the deer and the deer ate from her hand as it had from mine and it made no difference to it.

It's looking up at her face the way it used to look up to mine, I thought. It's letting her caress it.

MARITSA'S INTEREST LASTED two days. She stopped paying attention to the deer. She played with her toys and followed my mother around the house and sat opposite her at the table when my mother played solitaire and watched as she laid the worn cards on top of one another and said, "Th-th-three . . . se-ven . . . ace . . ." and my mother smiled and let her cut the deck after she shuffled. When we had people in the house and they asked to see the deer, Maritsa said, "The deer is mine," and went down to show it to them and hugged it, throwing her body over it, making it fall on the ground.

Manolis cut fresh branches for it and brought them home and dropped them by the basement door. When he got too busy with the summer chores, however, he asked my father if he could buy some grain for the deer instead, and my father said yes. He bought a burlap sack full of grain and put it in the basement and every day he gave the deer a fistful and changed its water.

No one paid attention to it now. No one cared. It grew sickly and thin, its fur pale like a fallen leaf. It had eaten all the grass and all the flowers and all the leaves it could reach and the garden was bare, rosebushes and briar standing among gray rocks and cracks on the parched ground, ghostly skeletons, gnarled and dark. It was as though the garden was dead, everything in it dead, and the deer, too, slowly dying. It did not run and traipse along and hop anymore. It sat under the apricot tree. Now and then it got on its legs and took a few steps and then sat down again.

When I came down, it tried to run to me—always it tried to run to me. I pushed it aside. I did not look at it. It suffered—I knew it suffered and hated it, despised it sometimes. It suffers like a weakling, I thought. It has no strength, no pride. I felt pain—a deep pain inside me. I did not want to feel pain. I did not want to care how the deer felt. I was angry at it. It's not mine anymore, I thought. My sister has fed it, my sister has touched it.

I wandered around the house restlessly.

"Bedeviled child," my mother said, "twirling about like the unjust curse. Get out of my sight! You're driving me crazy—crazy with your wandering about."

I went to the window and sat on the ledge. Manolis came behind me and looked over my shoulder.

"Anger that lasts and water that stands turn bad," he said.

"What does that mean?"

"You heard."

I turned and looked at him and he said:

"Go be with the deer."

"I don't want to."

"You want to, Annio. Don't torture your soul. You love it."

"Who says I love it?"

"Pride digs its own grave, stubbornness lays the tombstone."

"I don't know what you're saying."

"I'm saying go be with the deer."

"I said I won't have it back and I won't," I said. "When I say something I don't unsay it."

"Better unsay than undo."

ONE DAY AS we were sitting at the table at lunch Manolis came running up the stairs.

"Major, sir," he said. "The deer. I left the sack open. It got to it. It ate and drank water and—it's as good as gone, sir."

I jumped from my chair. Something bad has happened, I thought. Manolis is upset. Manolis is never upset.

"It was my fault, sir," he said. "I'm very sorry, sir."

"Any use calling the doctor?"

"No use, sir."

"Well, is it *dead*?" said my mother.

thought. I did not understand. My body understood, however. My body shook.

I ran to the basement.

Manolis came after me. He turned on the light.

The deer lay on its side, its belly bloated like a big pregnant beast's—a deer so small, sickly and fragile, a baby still, grotesquely dying. As always, as every time it saw me, it tried to come to me, it tried to get on its legs, kneeled and staggered. I reached for it and as I touched it, it licked my arm and looked up to my face. As it was looking at me, its eyes got dark and still.

"It's dead, Anna," Manolis said.

He held my shoulders and lifted me up.

All the love I had for it—the love I felt when I first held it, the love I felt when I loved it, the love I felt when I did not, the love I made myself not feel—all that love was not love. Now, now I felt love, and it was no good, it was no use now.

Manolis got a spade from the corner.

"Don't bury it—wait, wait! Maybe it isn't dead," I cried. "How do you know it's dead?"

"It's dead, Annoula. Touch its eyes and you'll see."

I touched my fingers on its eyes. They did not move. They were cold and sticky. It was horrid to touch them. It was horrible.

It was my last touch of it, the deer that had loved me blindly.

Little Wolf

THE NEW VILLAGE where we were stationed had sided with
the communists during the war. The reprisals had been hard.
To poverty had been added bitterness and humiliation, hate
and fear. The people were stern, silent, suffered from hunger
still. The children—barefoot, wearing their parents' old
clothes, patterns and colors faded to a uniform beige or gray,
boys with their heads shaved, girls in long braids—had
sunken cheeks, stooped bodies, calloused hands. Those whose
eyes did not look mean looked as though they would regard
evil with a leer.

When we moved into our house, they had stood outside
the garden and watched as the soldiers unloaded our things.
I came to the gate and smiled. They did not smile back.
They stared and watched and did not speak.

In the evening as I was coming home from the village
square, some of the boys followed from a distance and threw
stones at my feet. They did not aim to hit but to scare me.
One boy ran close and whispered behind my ear, "Security
Force, I like your cunt."

I walked faster.

"Where you going so fast, Security Force?" they called.
"Hey, Security Force! Security Force! Slow down. You'll
make us pant. Hey!"

"I don't want to go to school here," I said to my father
when I got home.

"This is where we'll live and this is where you'll go to
school for the next year."

"The children called me Security Force."

He laughed.

"How we pass our hatreds on to our children," my mother said. "Communists, rightists—all the spilled blood—and the hatred will go on unto the third generation."

"I don't hate the communists."

"You are not of an age to have opinions," said my father.

"Why is communism wrong?"

"Communists believe all people should be equal," he said. "People are not equal. Society is like your hand. Are all your fingers equal? No. Some are shorter and some are longer. If all your fingers were the same length, your hand would be useless. Society is the same thing. If all men were equal, society would not be able to function."

What did society have to do with my hand? I looked at my fingers.

"They are the same width," I said. "They are not fat and thin. The body gives them the same to eat."

My father shook his head.

"When you were two—only two," he said, "you had done some naughty thing—I forget what now—and you were trying to lie to me and explain how you hadn't done it. I told you I knew you were lying and I told you how. You said to me: 'Daddy, you are very intelligent. Bravo!' Now I say to you: 'Anna, you are very intelligent. Bravo!' "

"So communism *is* good?"

"As an idea, yes. Not in practice. Only a blackguard would not believe in communism in his youth and only a fool *would* believe in it after he's known life."

I did not understand. What is good is good, I thought. What is right, right.

My father said, "Don't worry about the children."

"They hate me."

"So they hate you," he said. "They say 'Friends show the

man.' Enemies show the man as well. But the true man—the true man shows himself. He doesn't care what others think or feel about him. He does what he must. A clear conscience fears no evil."

I did fear evil. If someone wants to do you evil, it's *their* conscience that can stop them, not yours, I thought. What good is a good conscience?

A FEW DAYS later, when I opened the door for my father as he was coming home, he asked me to close my eyes and hold my hands together palms up. "I have a surprise for you," he said.

He put something furry, squirming and wet in my hands. I opened my eyes and saw a small brown animal, its eyes closed and gummy, its ears pushed back, its mouth open, crying. My mother, Manolis and Maritsa came near to look.

"What is it?" asked my mother.

"A wolf."

"A wolf!" she said. "We have everything—only a wolf is missing in this house."

She started to laugh, she started to shake with laughter, and tears came to her eyes. "My God," she said. "My God, I think I'll go mad."

My father did not look at her.

"What do you know of wolves, Manoli?" he asked.

"They stay wild, major, sir," Manolis said. " 'You feed a wolf, his heart stays in the forest.' "

"This one came straight from the womb to human hands—it doesn't know of the forest."

"The blood speaks, major, sir."

"We'll see."

"We'll see? We'll see what?" my mother said. "Whether it will eat us?"

"Anna, what do you say?" my father said to me.

"What does *Anna* say?" my mother said. "What am *I* here?"

"Anna, do you want the wolf?" my father asked. "Anna, I'm talking to you."

"Yes."

"Madness!" my mother screamed. "Madness! The child is like you, mad."

"Shut up."

"This is my house, too. I won't have a wolf running around in my house. I'm telling you."

"I'm not asking. Anna, take the wolf in your room."

I took the little wolf to my room.

"Cursed be the day I met you," I heard my mother say. Then a door banged and there was silence. Manolis came in bringing a big carton and newspapers. He cut the paper in shreds, crumpled them and stuffed them in the carton.

"It may live and it may not," he said, looking at the wolf. "We'll have to feed it with an eye-dropper for now."

"I thought wolves were black."

"It'll turn black."

"I thought wolves had big ears."

"It'll have big ears."

"And big teeth?"

"And big teeth."

"Will it eat me, you think?"

Manolis was silent.

"They have lions that are tame in the circus."

"I don't know what they have in the circus, I."

"They have lions and tigers and elephants in the circus."

"I don't know about tigers and elephants, I. The wolf is an enemy to man."

"Why?"

"It has a black soul—that's why."

"Do you know about Romulus and Remus?"

"No."

I told him about Romulus and Remus and the kind she-wolf that fed them.

"I don't know about Romulus and Remus, I. I know what I know."

The wolf curled in my lap, its fur fluffy and mussy, coarse to touch like unspun wool—a sleepy baby creature, warm and soft under my hand. He's not going to eat me, I thought. I'll be his mama. A child doesn't eat his mama.

The wolf ate and slept at first and did not move much or make a sound, then it started to scamper out of its box and scurry to and fro and did not stand still. It did not play and it did not like to be cuddled. It let me hold it when I fed it, but when I tried to pet it, it bit my hand. At night, when I turned the light out and went to bed, it stood in the middle of the room and howled, its howls filling the house and echoing in the night, loud, desperate. It's crying, "I'm alone . . . *unhappy . . .*" I thought.

My mother said, "I'll go mad. I'll go mad with that sound."

I took the wolf in my bed and held it to make it stop, but the wolf bit me and growled and fought to get out of my hands like a bird that, trying to open its wings and fly free, trembles in a fist, frantic. It burrowed under the covers and stayed in the corner at the foot of the bed. Later, as I lay still trying to go to sleep, it crawled along my leg and crept under my nightgown, climbed on my belly and lay with its snout wet on my skin, wheezing softly as though crying. I couldn't touch it. As soon as I touched it, it bit.

It isn't meanness, I thought. He's grouchy, like boys moving away, scowling when grown-ups fondle and kiss them. Boys did not like caresses. They bristled and became edgy and looked at you with sullen sidelong glances.

The wolf was like that, I thought.

.   .   .

THE FIRST DAY in school the teacher said we should not pick
up loose metal from the ground for there were landmines
and hand-grenades that had not exploded and would if we
touched them—even lightly with the tips of our fingers. She
called a boy named Stavros who had one arm blown to the
wrist and the other with only the thumb and little finger left
on it to come in front of the class and show us his deformi-
ties.

"Same thing will happen to you," she said.

Stavros put his one crippled hand in his pocket, swaggered
to his seat, leaned back on his desk and smiled as though to
say, "I do what I want—I'm maimed and I'm mean." The rest
of us had to keep our hands on top of the desk, fingers
entwined, and sit with our backs straight, leaning forward.

The teacher said, "One more thing before we start the
year. We must all be nice to Vaggelio. Her mother is sick
and dying."

She did not ask Vaggelio to get up but everyone turned
and looked at her and Vaggelio bent her head down.

She is the girl next door, I thought. She is the girl of the
woman dying in the beautiful garden.

Vaggelio's father used to drink and beat her mother and
had deserted them when Vaggelio was four. He went to
Thessaloniki and worked no one knew at what. Her mother
had tuberculosis that was in its final stages. She embroidered
to make money and on good days lay on a mattress in the
garden and worked from morning till the sun went down.

Their house was old, with broken shutters and moss
growing on the walls, half hidden by shrubbery and wild
vines and weeds. Manolis said, looking at it, "Shows there's
no man."

If there were a man, the house would stand whitewashed

and bare, I thought. The garden would be weeded, empty. In other houses, where there lived men, the soil was hard and dry, swept clean. Men do not like things to grow unless they plant them, I thought. It's good there's no man. The garden is like Paradise now. Paradise must be like that, I thought. God did not have Paradise pruned. I was sure of it. God liked all things that grew.

Vaggelio's mother lay still, only her hands moving, moving tirelessly, incessant, filling the white cloth amassed in her lap with glimmering silk, bright yellow, red, pink, green, a pattern of flowers and leaves, as though beauty flowed from her hands—a silent song like a swan's. She lay with her hair loose on the pillow, her cheeks red, her eyes shining.

I had seen swans in a lake once. They were alive swans. They were swimming, not dying. They croaked and their voices were ugly. Maybe when they die, their voices become beautiful and they sing nicely. The woman's work was beautiful and her hands were beautiful and her face was beautiful and everything in her garden was beautiful.

Vaggelio, too, is beautiful, I thought.

She was a tall, stocky girl with blue eyes and thick blond hair, brown sunburned skin and big pale lips, mauve like cyclamens but undelicate, fleshy, firm, half open as though hungry—an avid mouth that had been denied pleasure, already having hard lines at the sides. Her eyes had a deep, steady gaze that fixed on your face wistfully but seemed to look beyond you.

She is like a poplar, I thought, strong and tall, alone silver-white among dark green trees.

"The girl next door is called Vaggelio," I said to Manolis when I got home. "She's like a poplar."

Manolis sat on the porch whittling a stick with his pocket knife. He nodded without looking at me.

"You're like a plane tree," I said to him.

Manolis nodded again.

"A *young* plane tree."

Manolis looked up. "What tree are you?" he said.

"I'm not a tree."

"What are you?"

"I don't know what I am."

Manolis swished the stick in the air and put the knife in his pocket.

I said, "The wolf is like a fire. A bonfire on top of a mountain that burns in the night."

"*I* know what you are. A little cloud."

"White?"

"Yes. White."

I had never thought I was a cloud. I looked at the sky to see if there were any clouds but there were no clouds.

"Where do clouds go when they're not in the sky?"

"Under the earth," he said. "To the other side."

I didn't want to be something that left the face of the earth. I didn't want to be high up, apart from the world, touching nothing. I got sick when I was high up. I don't want to be a cloud, I thought. Why is Manolis saying I'm a cloud?

VAGGELIO SAT TWO desks behind me. I could not see her when we were in class but I was happy thinking, Vaggelio is in this room, Vaggelio is copying down the same sentence, Vaggelio is turning the same page now.

Because my mother gave me food to eat in school, at recess I wasn't allowed to go out in the yard. The teacher said:

"If you want to eat, eat inside."

"In my other school—"

"In your other school the children had food to eat. This is poor country. You stay in the classroom."

"I'm not hungry. I won't eat."

"You *will* eat. Your mother gave you food to eat and you should eat it. But not in front of children who are hungry."

She made me sit down and eat as though food were punishment, asking each day, "What have we this time? Butter and sugar? Butter and cheese? Good. Eat it."

She sat at her desk and watched me eat.

When I was done I climbed to the window and looked at Vaggelio sitting in the yard alone, the other girls walking up and down arm in arm laughing and talking, the boys chasing each other and fighting.

Every day I wanted to say "I love you, Vaggelio," but could not say it. People don't say "I love you" without warning. We had never talked. I have to say something else first, I thought. What can I say first? I couldn't think of anything that did not sound stupid and silly. How can I say "I love you, Vaggelio" after I've just said something stupid and silly?

I said it inside me—I love you, Vaggelio . . . I love you, Vaggelio . . . It made me sad to say it inside me. Vaggelio looked sad, too. Was she saying "I love you, Anna" inside her?

We walked back from school slowly, quietly, without saying a word. When we reached her house, Vaggelio stopped with her back to their gate, her arm behind her, her hand on the latch and waited looking at me till I got to our gate, then ran inside calling "Mama! Mama!"

She took care of their house, chopping wood, carrying water from the well, lighting the fire—everything strenuous for the mother, her child's body muscular, coarse-skinned from work, exhausted.

At night, when it was quiet and the sound carried far, we heard the woman cough and retch blood. Sometimes she coughed all night.

"I don't see how that poor child sleeps," said my father.

Their house was one small room. I had gone in to see Vaggelio once when I was sick and had missed school.

My mother had said:

"Don't touch anything. Don't let them touch you. Don't eat if they offer you something. Don't catch the disease. Careful."

The only furniture was a trunk, a table where you had to sit on the floor to eat and two mattresses. A frying pan, a clay pot, a tin kettle, a few plates and cups were stacked on the fireplace ledge. There was a kerosene lamp on the table and an icon stand mounted on the wall. Vaggelio's books were piled on the floor next to her bed mattress. It was damp and airless, the walls covered with soot from the fire, the icon blackened—the face of Our Lady scary, featureless under the halo.

Vaggelio squatted on the floor peeling potatoes.

"You got well," she said.

"Get up and greet your friend," her mother said. "What manner is this?"

Even when they're dying, mothers scold, I thought.

Vaggelio obeyed.

How could she have such beautiful eyes and live in a place like this? Eyes were beautiful, I thought, from looking at beautiful things. People were beautiful from living among beautiful things. Maybe it's the opposite, I thought. Maybe if you have beautiful eyes, you see things beautiful even when they are ugly. I didn't have beautiful eyes. I had intelligent eyes. Everyone said I had intelligent eyes. "What intelligent eyes she has!" they said. If I had beautiful eyes like Vaggelio's everything I saw would be beautiful. I would be happy. I wasn't happy as I was. Only when I was near Vaggelio did I feel happy. When I was near Vaggelio, unhappy felt like happy.

"When I'm near you, unhappy is like happy, Vaggelio," I wanted to say. No one says such things, I thought.

"What's for homework?" I said.

Vaggelio showed me.

"Good-bye now."

"Good-bye."

She walked with me to the garden gate. She must think I'm beautiful with her beautiful eyes, I thought. Vaggelio sees me beautiful!

VAGGELIO'S MOTHER DIED in early spring. We saw the priest go to the house at night and, the next day, the village women come and take Vaggelio's clothes and dye them black and hang them out to dry. The sun shone bright and flowers filled the yard, red, yellow, white, pink, like the flowers the dead woman had sewn. Vaggelio's wet clothes swayed in the breeze dripping black dye.

In the afternoon a man with a horsecart drove to the house. Slowly the village children gathered around it, watching in silence, their eyes transfixed, gloating on misery that did not touch them.

Vaggelio ran out of the house screaming, "You won't take her. No! No! I want my mama back. I want my mama."

The women tried to calm her. They brought her water to drink and whispered to her and hugged her.

The driver hit the horse and the cart started rattling on the stony road, Vaggelio walking alone behind it, the women following at a distance, their heads bent, crying.

The church bells tolled all evening.

I sat on the porch steps with my head in my hands.

"Poor girl," Manolis said. "No greater unhappiness than a motherless child."

Vaggelio did not come back to school. They had written her father in Thessaloniki and he would come and take her to live with him and she would go to school there. A cousin of her mother's—Gethsemani the Twin—came to sleep with Vaggelio at night so Vaggelio would not sleep alone but in the day went back to her own house.

She packed her clothes in a bundle and every day came out and sat on a tree stump in the garden and waited for her father, the bundle on the ground by her feet, her eyes fixed on the road.

When I passed her house coming from school, she looked away and did not greet me. She's thinking of her dead mother, I thought. I'm nothing to her in her grief. She doesn't even want to look at me.

I went home, to my room, and took the wolf in my lap. The wolf bit me. The more he bit me, the more I caressed him and cuddled him. He's the only thing I have, I thought. He'll love me in time.

ONE DAY I was walking in the village and saw a house covered with jasmine. The door was open and I went in to tell the people who lived there I liked their jasmine.

There was a man reading a book and a woman knitting a sock inside.

"I like your jasmine," I said.

The man looked up from his book and the woman lowered the sock in her lap.

"She's the major's daughter," she said to the man.

"What's your name?" he said.

"Anna."

"Well, Anna . . . Come in."

He had long messy hair and tired, blood-rimmed eyes. He must read a lot, I thought. He must be an unusual peasant. Peasants don't read. There was a small bookcase made of crate wood against the wall filled with big thick books. Cousin Mary read books that looked like that. She read with her head close to the book, scowling. Cousin Mary read to make herself wise. She said things like, "Pygmies in Africa are one meter tall," and "The Eskimos kiss with their nose."

"I like books with dialogue in them," I said.

The man nodded.

"I'll be a writer when I grow up."

"What will you write about?"

"About knights."

The man smiled.

"What's the book you're reading?"

"*The Rise of the Proletarians.*"

"What's proletarians?"

"They are the poor of the world united against injustice."

"Which injustice?"

"The rich sucking their blood."

"Like in *Oliver Twist?*"

"Like in life."

The proletarians must be a secret society like the Masons, I thought. Cousin Mary had told me about the Masons.

"You've already read *Oliver Twist?*"

"I've read it in the Illustrated Classics. I read all the Illustrated Classics. I have a grown-up uncle who reads them and sends them to me after he's done. His name is Menelaos but he's called The Ox."

The man smiled again. He had a sad but kindly smile. I noticed a copy of *The Sunrise* by his feet, read and thrown crumpled on the floor. He's a communist, I thought. Is he a fool as my father says communists are who have known life and still keep their beliefs? He had known life, I could tell, for he had wrinkles on his face and eyes that asked questions as though giving the answer—as though they knew what you'd say, the way my father's gave silent commands knowing you'd obey. My father's eyes were fierce and fiery, the man's tired and gentle. They looked like my uncle Christos' whose boy "the Alekaki" had leukemia and died when he was five, his liver big as a melon in his stomach and his round eyes staring in pain on his small pale face. Uncle Christos held no grudge against God and continued to pray, as though the Alekaki was still alive. Perhaps the man holds on to his beliefs as Uncle Christos holds on to praying, I thought.

The woman went out, cut two twigs of jasmine and gave them to me. "That's so you remember us," she said.

"Oh, I remember everyone I meet. Thank you."

Vaggelio saw me come home with the jasmine and did not look away. She did not look away but she did not smile either. I went to the fence and stood outside the garden and we looked at each other and did not speak. After a while, Vaggelio came to the fence and said, "Where did you get the jasmine?"

I told her about the man who read books and his wife.

"The Kontopoulei," she said. "She's not from our parts, the wife. He brought her from Thessaloniki, he did, where he had gone to be a doctor. He was going to be a doctor, Kontopoulis was."

"Why didn't he become one?"

"With the war . . . I don't know . . ."

"What does he do now?"

"Farms his father's land. He was rich, his father was. Kontopoulis was my uncle's friend—my uncle that was killed. He was a communist, my uncle. He asked my father to hide him when they were hunting them afterward and my father turned him out. 'Go to those you killed and ask for help,' my

father said. They found him in the threshing field and shot
him there, by the oak. He's a bad man, my father is. No one
talks to him in the village—no, they don't. My mother
didn't talk to him either. He beat her but she didn't talk. He
was my mother's brother, that uncle. She had another
brother—the Germans killed him. My aunt is in Rumania."

"Doesn't your father have relatives here?"

"They're in America, my father's family. We were going
to go, too, but we couldn't go on account of my mother
being sick. They don't take you in America if you're sick,
that they don't. In Russia they take you. They pay for doctors in Russia and put you in a nice hospital there, they do."

"May I come in, Vaggelio?"

"Come in, do."

We sat side by side on the tree stump and Vaggelio talked
and talked. How suddenly it happened—just when I had
given up all hope! Vaggelio had never talked before and now
she talked and couldn't stop. It wouldn't have happened if I
didn't have the jasmine in my hands and she hadn't asked me
where I got it. It wouldn't have happened if I hadn't taken a
walk and seen the house and stopped. What if I had not gone
that way?

"Death is waiting to take me, he is," Vaggelio said. "He'll
take me as he took my mother, he will. I hear him."

"How can you hear him?"

"I hear him at night, I do, as when my mother was dying.
He howls like a wolf."

"It *is* a wolf, Vaggelio. It's my wolf!"

I ran to the house and brought the wolf.

"It's a wolf, that?"

"He's a baby. When he grows he'll turn black and he'll
have big ears and big teeth. See? You won't die."

"Don't he bite?"

"Only if you touch him."

I put the wolf in her lap and he curled up and stayed quiet.

"Do you want to be friends, Vaggelio?"

"Yes."

"Best friends?"

"Yes."

"When is your father coming?"

"I don't know . . . He'll come . . ."

"I don't want him to come. You'll go away then."

"He has to come. He has to. Who'll take me in if he doesn't come?"

Every day after school I went to Vaggelio's now and sat close to her on the tree stump holding her hand. It was like saying good-bye, a long good-bye lasting all day, beginning again the next day and the next.

THE DAYS PASSED and Vaggelio's father had not come. The wolf got bigger. His teeth got sharp. His teeth now hurt me when he bit me. They cut the skin and drew blood and made small holes where they bit. I held my hands behind my back to hide them, walking swaying on my feet, the way people do when they stroll carefree and whistle, and made like I was happy so my mother would not notice. But my mother said:

"What's this new thing? What do you mean walking like that? Stop it. And stop smiling like an idiot."

I went to my room and put on my red velvet dress that had pockets in the skirt and came out again with my hands in the pockets.

"Why did you put your good dress on?" my mother said. "Have you gone wrong in the head? I ask you!"

I didn't answer.

We sat at the table and waited for my father to come home for lunch.

I can't eat with my hands in my pockets, I thought. How will I eat? I'll wear my gloves.

When my father came home and Manolis started serving the meal, I excused myself, went to my room and put on my gloves.

My mother looked at me as if I had grown two heads.

"This is too much," she said. "This is the end! Stephane, she went and put gloves on."

My father shrugged and started to eat.

I sat down and picked up my fork.

"Put the fork down and take off your gloves," my mother said. "You're not going to eat with your gloves on. No one eats with their gloves on."

"There's no rule against it."

"There's no rule against people wearing feathers on their head but I don't see anyone wearing them."

"Indians do."

"We're not Indians. Stop retorting."

She reached across the table, took my hand and pulled the glove off. The scabs had caught on the wool and the wounds tore open and bled.

"What happened to your hand? *What happened to your hand?*" she screamed. "Let me see your other one."

I showed my other hand.

"Stephane! Stephane, will you stop eating and look at her hands? They're mangled."

"They're not mangled," I said. "They have small little bites."

"My God, I have a husband who brings wolves home and a child who feeds them her flesh. I'll go mad! I'll go mad!" she said.

My father put iodine on my hands and covered them with bandages, then called Manolis and told him to take the wolf with him to the barracks when he left that night.

"It's not his fault, Daddy. He doesn't want me to touch him. He didn't attack—he doesn't."

"You don't bite the hand that feeds you," he said. "You don't bite the hand that feeds you even if it's trying to kill you. It's a human and animal law that."

"What will you do?"

"Shoot him."

"Let him free in the forest, Daddy."

"He had his chance. Eat up!"

After lunch I ran to Vaggelio's and told her my father was going to shoot the wolf.

Vaggelio put her arms around me and hugged me.

My mother saw us hugging each other and screamed, "Anna! Anna!"

I went upstairs and she dragged me inside by the sleeve.

"Were you kissing Vaggelio?" she said.

"No."

"Swear you haven't kissed her."

"I swear."

"What were you doing with her?"

"I wasn't doing anything with her."

"Why are you crying?"

"I'm not crying."

"I saw you hugging her."

"I hugged her. What's wrong if I hugged her?"

"What's wrong if you hugged her! The girl's mother died tubercular. The girl may have it, too—if she doesn't she's a carrier. Answer me this: Do you want to get sick and cough blood? Do you want to die? I'm asking: Do you want to die?"

Later that afternoon, Manolis came to my room to take the wolf.

"Little Cloud, don't be sad," he said. "The wolf is no friend to man."

"He *is* my friend."

"Little Cloud, don't cry. It's bad to love what can't love back. I'm unlearned, I. You got sense and knowledge though only a child. You don't want to have a foolish heart. The heart must be wise—it must love what can love."

I RAN TO Vaggelio's. The door of the house was open and I walked inside. Vaggelio was napping, lying on the mattress in a black slip, her braids loose, her blond hair golden on her brown body, the black rags she used to tie at the end of her braids on the edge of her pillow, stretched neatly side by side. They've dyed everything of hers black except her hair, I thought. Her hair is like sunlight in dark shadows.

I sat on the mattress and whispered her name to wake her.

Vaggelio sat up, frightened.

"They've taken Little Wolf away. They're going to kill him."

Vaggelio lay down on the mattress again and closed her eyes.

I felt desperate. No one—even Vaggelio—wanted to see Little Wolf couldn't help himself when he bit; he wasn't mean—it was all he knew to do. When he bit me, the pain was like feeling the pain he felt inside him. When he hurt me, it was like he was saying, Love me more—love me! It was terrifying to speak the love that was in one's heart. But one must, I thought. One must, or who one loves will go away or die.

"Vaggelio, talk to me. Don't go back to sleep."

Vaggelio looked at me, her eyes heavy with sleep, and nudged her face on my arm.

"Talk about what?"

"Remember when we first knew each other how we didn't talk?"

"I remember."

"Did you want to talk?"

"Yes."

"Me too. I wanted to say, 'Vaggelio, I love you.' Vaggelio . . ."

She put her hand over my mouth. She kissed me on my forehead and, taking her hand away, on my nose and lips. She kissed my mouth and opened it and kissed the lips inside. Now I'll die, I thought. The sickness is on me. I'll die.

ONE DAY A car drove to Vaggelio's house. It had patches of sheet metal and primer, missing headlights, sockets gaping open, fenders beat-in and creased. A man in a dark shiny suit and hat low over the eyes came out. He wore a handkerchief in his breast pocket and a ring on his hand, the nail on the little finger long and filed. He had a short mustache and gold teeth that he bared in a slow sly smile, his eyes not changing expression. He stood with one foot over the other, legs crossed, leaning on the car with his arm on the door. He looked Vaggelio up and down, then pushed his hat to the back of his head and said, "Got your things?"

Vaggelio got up. She looked frightened. She did not move.

"Is that your father?"

"He must be."

"Come on. Come on," the man said. "I can't drive this thing at night. I don't have time to waste."

Vaggelio picked up the bundle with her clothes and walked toward him, her body bent to the side from the weight.

"Vaggelio!" I shouted, running after her. "Vaggelio, wait."

Just then my mother came home from the market, Manolis following behind her carrying the things she had bought.

The man took off his hat and bowed. My mother nodded and went inside.

"Good-bye, Anna," Vaggelio said. "Remember me."

"I won't forget you, Vaggelio. I'll never forget you!"

We put our arms around each other and kissed.

"Anna!" my mother screamed. "Anna!"

She stood halfway up the porch stairs looking down at me, shaking.

I waited till Vaggelio got in the car and the car left, then went up to her.

"What have you done, demon?" she said. "Why are you seeking disaster? Why do you go knowingly to your ruin? Who kisses a tubercular, my God? Who kisses a tubercular?"

Manolis had put down the groceries and was watching us.

"Wash her face," my mother said to him. "Don't just stand there. Wash her face with soap."

Manolis took me to the kitchen and washed my face.

"Her mouth, too," my mother said, standing behind us.

Manolis washed my lips.

"Inside!" my mother said. "Inside!"

Manolis put the soap inside my mouth. I gagged and I wanted to vomit—wanted to vomit the love I felt for Vaggelio.

"And change her bandages," my mother said.

She left.

Manolis untied the bandages and took my hands in his.

"Almost healed, Little Cloud," he said. "Wounds mend and scars don't hurt. Pain lasts as long as it lasts, then lo! It isn't there."

Bitch

A TIME WE were in Athens on a short visit my father bought a German shepherd. It was a female dog. His cousin Ekavi, who had lost her parents in the Asia Minor Disaster, was brought up by Grandpa Damien and lived in his house till she left to live with her friend Elisavetta, a failed actress whom she supported by working in a bank and giving French lessons at night—a fact well-known in the family but unacknowledged as though Ekavi had no existence outside the christenings and weddings and formal gatherings where she unfailingly materialized like an official compelled to attend a ceremony hiding neither his boredom nor disdain—this Ekavi, coming to the party Grandpa gave for the family in honor of our visit, upon seeing the puppy, said to my father, "You *would* get a bitch." As was usually the case when she said something, the conversation came to an abrupt stop and resumed in a self-conscious, haltering tone, like actors rehearsing.

She was in her forties, a stately, handsome woman with sallow skin, thick dark hair and a wide mouth that would look generous if the lips were not closed tight as though to suppress constant pain—suffering and bitterness marking the defiant rigidness of her bearing.

Grandpa had treated her no different than his children and had special affection for her, having loved her mother, his sister. But his wife, with seven children of her own, resented the extra child and showed it. Ekavi kept to herself. She worked assiduously at school, to the limit of her powers, yet showed no joy at coming first, accepting honors and

prizes with indifference—the barren satisfaction of someone
giving all he has to repay his debts. In total command of her
will, in her life having always, implacably, exerted her best,
she had a condescending confidence, antagonizing assurance
and severity, her eyes seeming continually to pass judgment,
not harsh but weary, as though sure of disappointment.
Around her friend Elisavetta, she was thoughtful, quiet, her
gestures and smile gentle, soft, humble even, her gaze when
she looked at her like a man's come to shore, looking at the
horizon hem the sea, standing still, serene.

The members of the family regarded Ekavi with disap-
proval and civil dislike. Elisavetta beyond being called
mockingly "the artista" was not discussed.

One time when I was little and my mother and Aunt
Ermioni had taken me to the fair, Elisavetta and Aunt Ekavi
came toward us as we were walking. They stopped to greet
us. Aunt Ekavi did not smile but Elisavetta smiled and said,
excited, "Have you seen the severed head that speaks?" She
wore white and was beautiful and had blond hair that my
mother said was dyed and looked "cheap," as she had said of
the bracelet I wanted her to buy me that had shiny red
stones. How can something beautiful be cheap? I thought.
What a thing to say, "I won't buy it—it's cheap!" She had
dragged me away from the jewelry stand and now she dragged
me away from Elisavetta saying to Aunt Ermioni, "Cheap!
She's cheap!"

How can a person be cheap? When I grow up, I'll dye my
hair and wear red stones and be cheap and beautiful like
Elisavetta.

"I want to see the severed head!"

"It's a stupid trick. Come along," my mother said. She
said to Aunt Ermioni, "I don't know what it adds to a child's
education taking them to fairs. Perverts their minds, I
think."

"What does 'perverts' mean?"

"Twists."

"The mind can twist?"

"When it thinks twisted thoughts."

"If I see the severed head, my mind will twist?"

"Yes . . ."

"Why?"

"Because you'll start thinking heads without bodies can speak."

"Won't it untwist after?"

"No."

"Why?"

"Because it doesn't know better."

She took me to see the baboon that stood on the gypsy's arm. The baboon had a bald ass and kept showing it to us. I didn't want to see the baboon's ass. I wanted to see the severed head.

"I want to see the severed head!"

"Anna, you behave yourself, or you'll see nothing."

"I want to see the severed head! I want to see the severed head!"

They led me home, my mother on one side, Aunt Ermioni on the other, screaming all the way, "I want to twist my mind! I want to see the severed head! I want to twist my mind! I want to see the severed head!"

"What happened?" asked my aunts when we were in the house.

"We ran into Guess-Who," Aunt Ermioni said.

"Who?"

"The cousin and company. They started her on this."

"They did! *What* is she *screaming*?"

"She wants to see the severed head—she wants to twist her mind."

"Well, I never!"

But I did see the severed head. I saw the severed head in my sleep. First it was a man's head that had black hair with lots and lots of brilliantine on it and stuck to his scalp. Then it was a woman's head that had wild crinkly hair with gold-dust on it. It stood on end and sparkled and sparked.

The head was cut at the neck. It had been cut by a saw. The skin had red blood festoons at the end. The eyes were glass. They were like a doll's eyes. The mouth was open. The mouth had loose teeth—they dangled in it. A snake slid behind the teeth. It moved the teeth back and forth, back and forth. Then the teeth fell out. The mouth swallowed them, then opened again. There was no blood. The snake was a tongue now. It was pink and soft. I woke up.

I related my dream at the table and Grandpa Damien said, "The Medusa head turned angelic. I wonder what Freud would say to that."

"You can't protect a child's innocence enough," said Uncle Thanasis. He was married to my father's sister Vasilia, was a civil servant, a man of exaggerated dignity, puritanical morals, supercilious irony. He had no tolerance for argument, reacting to dissent as to affrontery: lips pressed like an old maid's savoring her prudery and bile.

"My dear Thanasi, 'innocence' is a creed like the Immaculate Conception," said Grandpa. "You believe in one, you certainly must believe in the other. Sex exerts its influence from the cradle to the grave. To call sex a sin is to think life a travesty and make hypocrisy a pleasure. I'd rather, like the ancients, believe in virtue. Virtue is proven, not bargained for with some priest."

"The ancients discounted the soul."

"A people whose genius created the Parthenon and the *Iliad* surely did not discount the soul. The soul of Greece lives in every civilized man's thought."

"A man's spirit is not the same as a man's soul."

"Perhaps. Perhaps. But you can't argue it comes into being without sex. You venerate the soul, venerate its *prima causa.*" He laughed. "Much as the Greeks despised women, they respected Venus. . . . They gave the words 'life' and 'soul' the female gender. To death, the masculine gender. It should give us pause, that."

"Are we discussing linguistics? I wasn't aware."

"Linguistics! It's the language you speak, man! Speak it every day."

" 'Paradise' is masculine may I remind you then."

"Yes," said Grandpa. "So is 'the evil serpent.' "

"What are you saying?"

"I'm saying: Life is good, sex is good, and sin the creation of the arrogant impotence of the male unable to rule Nature. Unable to rule Woman, if it comes to that."

"Father Bluestocking," Aunt Despo said.

Grandpa laughed. "It's humbling for a man to have a daughter," he said. "I had six. I'm a humble man—a humble man is wise."

"You forget your son. A good thing he isn't present," Uncle Thanasis said.

"No, I don't forget my son. I'm proud of my son. But a son doesn't show us ourselves. It takes a daughter to show us the meanness of our sex. Have a daughter and love her and try to see her with other men's eyes and see what you think of men."

"As you well know, I do have one. A woman gets the look she invites."

"You don't love her then."

"Mary is an excellent girl. I certainly do love her. . . . 'The meanness of our sex'! May I remind you of the oldest profession? And that through the ages it's been the only profession women have been known to hold with success?"

"So? Is the man going to a prostitute worthier than she? It's of his baseness she avails. Sex is a woman's privilege and power."

"The privilege to submit to man."

"It's we who submit, my dear. It's we—as every honest man knows."

Uncle Thanasis pressed his lips and did not answer.

I asked my aunts later, "What's a pra-sta-tute?"

"Nothing."

"What's sex?"

"Nothing."

"Why doesn't Elisavetta come see us when Aunt Ekavi comes?"

"She's busy."

"What does she do?"

"Nothing."

All the words grown-ups say are "nothing" mean the same thing, I thought.

I went to the kitchen and watched Elengo peel potatoes. She peeled the skin, then threw the potatoes in a big basin of water. I climbed on a chair and stood on the seat to see them go *plop plop.* When the last potato was in, Elengo took the basin to the sink. I sat down on the chair, rested my elbows on the table and held my chin.

My mother came in holding two aspirins in her hand.

"Elengo, a glass of water," she said. "I have a headache, I could kill." She shook my shoulder and said, "Sit like a human being. I've told you it's bad to hold your chin."

"Why?"

"You'll get a jut-jaw—that's why."

When she left, I held my chin in my hands again.

"You must listen to your mother, child," Elengo said. "Don't sit like that. It's bad luck. Man hangs his head down without reason, the reason is soon to come. It's not for a child to be grave and sad."

I didn't move.

"You mustn't think sad thoughts, Annio. Every time you think of something sad and hold your chin like that, your chin will grow a little bigger. Would you like to have a chin out to here?"

Like Pinocchio's nose! I thought. I put my hands down frightened.

I had a chin that grew! I was not like other children. I must have been ready-made. I wasn't born by my mama. Mama had explained to me how babies are born. I had asked:

"How did Maritsa come out from inside your belly, Mama?"

"Women have a hole in their bellies," she said.

"Where?"

"Between the legs."

"You have a hole between your legs? As big as Maritsa? Oh, Mama!"

"It's a small hole. Small-small."

"How can the baby come out then—if the hole is small-small?"

"It pushes and the hole stretches out. How does the egg come out of the chicken? Have you seen chickens lay eggs?"

She means the asshole, I thought. I'd seen chickens. Sure, I'd seen chickens.

I looked at my feet shame-faced.

"Are all babies born like this, or only Maritsa?"

"All."

She means Maritsa and other children. Not me, I thought. When you say bad things about people to a person, you are saying, "*You* are not like that. *You* are different." You don't *say* it, but that's what you mean. You would not say to a person, "People come out of their mamas' assholes," if that person came out of an asshole, too.

Mama is telling me this as a secret, I thought. It's between her and me. We're friends, Mama and I.

Elengo put a plate with a piece of cake on it in front of me.

"Now, we're talking," she said. "That's a real smile. What I like to see."

I am like Pinocchio, I thought, as I ate the cake. I wasn't born, I was made. I have a chin that grows big when I pout and gets small when I smile.

I held my nose and said to Elengo, "I'm one hundred years old."

My nose stayed put. I can lie if I want to, I thought. All my good fairy wishes is that I be cheerful.

Elengo smiled.

"Elengo, are you my good fairy?"

"Yes," she said. "You're a hundred years old and I'm your good fairy. More cake?"

"Why didn't my good fairy tell me herself about my chin? Why did she have *you* tell me?"

"She did not want to come to the house. Fairies don't go calling."

It's Elisavetta, I thought. Elisavetta! She never goes calling. She is beautiful, as fairies are, and has gold hair and blue eyes, as fairies do, and wears silver sandals without heels. My mother always wore heels. My aunts wore loafers and bobby socks. Only fairies wore heel-less silver shoes.

When Aunt Ekavi came to say good-bye to us before we left Grandpa's, I climbed in her lap and whispered, "Tell Elisavetta I'm cheerful."

"I will."

"See my chin?"

"I see your chin."

"It hasn't grown one bit. You tell her."

"What is she saying?" asked Grandpa.

"Her chin hasn't grown one bit, she says."

"She'll say anything to talk," my father said.

But Aunt Ekavi understood. She put her arms around me and whispered back, "I'll tell her. She'll be happy."

AT THE PARTY, Aunt Ekavi said, "You *would* get a bitch," to my father, and my father, looking away from her and in a loud voice addressing everyone in the room, said, "I always choose the female sex. I had two daughters, didn't I?"

Aunt Vasilia, sitting in the big chair, her feet on extra cushions on the ottoman to ease her varicose veins, said unaccountably, "Show me a scarecrow, I'll show you a smart crow. If you catch a thief once, you won't catch him twice."

There was a silence, then Cousin Mary supplemented her mother's comment saying, "The Muslims cut a thief's hand at the wrist."

Aunt Vasilia was irritable and bossy, Mary even-tempered and pedantic. She divulged this jarring information with a placid smile, her forefinger primly pushing up her glasses.

There was a new silence.

"When will the joyful event be, Ermioni?" said my mother.

"There will be no joyful event," Ermioni said. "I refused him."

"Why, Ermioni, he has tons of money."

"I'm not for sale."

"Women who are not for sale end up renting out," my father said.

"Or owning their bodies," said Aunt Ekavi.

"For the good that does them," answered my father without looking at her. "Ermioni, you're kicking your luck."

"I *said* I don't want him."

Ermioni left the room and banged the door behind her.

"Temper! Temper!" said Uncle Thanasis.

"The way she doesn't take care of her appearance, it's a wonder the man noticed her, let alone proposed," said Aunt Vasilia.

"Mr. Papageorgiou has astigmatism," said Cousin Mary. "I've read that most astigmatism is psychosomatic. Like other neurotics, astigmatics are sensitive and idiosyncratic. Besides, they can't see. I've read—"

"Ermioni is a good soul," Aunt Maro interrupted. "A worthy man looks beyond the appearance."

"The only place such worthy men are found is in the minds of unattractive women," said my father. "When a man wants to fuck a woman, he wants to fuck her body. Her soul may be worth a thousand saints' but that won't get his pecker up."

"Stephane, there are children here!" shouted Aunt Vasilia.

"We know what fuck means, Mother."

"Mary!"

"Unattractive women do marry," said Aunt Despo.

"And whorehouses stay in business."

"You're not *all* men, Stephane."

"No. But if there's one thing I know, it's men."

Aunt Ekavi said, "No doubt. You make an excellent case for them." She got up and picked up her hat. "You'll permit me to leave. I find this conversation offensive."

"Of course," my father said. " 'The artista' is waiting . . ."

"I don't feel one way or the other about my propensity," said Aunt Ekavi. "Around men like you, however, it seems a privilege. Good-bye."

No one said good-bye back and no one got up. Grandpa looked down at the floor. The others stared in front of them in silence. Aunt Ekavi stood hat in hand for a moment then left the house unseen to the door.

.   .   .

UNLIKE GRANDPA DAMIEN who spoke meditatively—his statements weighed, carrying the conviction of explored argument—or other men who defended their opinions jealously as though truth were a personal claim and its compromise a compromise of honor, my father spoke his mind like a man who speaks the law. In the army you command, not convince. This attitude he carried into life and people bowed to it. His words were respected, his anger unopposed, his madness not reasoned against. Once he drove our car two kilometers on a flooded road where the lake had overflowed. Uncle Stavros, in the car with us, said in disbelief as he saw us heading for the water, "We're not going in, are we?"

"Cars are amphibian," my father said laughing.

Uncle Stavros acquiesced.

The car waded slowly through the lake. Dead fish floated on the surface of the water all around us. Why did the flood kill the fish? I thought. How can too much water kill a fish? I didn't think it strange we were driving in a car through a lake. Only the dead fish seemed strange.

"We'll never make it across," Uncle Stavros said. "How do you know you're keeping on the road? Why are we doing this? It's likely we'll drown."

"We said we would go to the inn for coffee," my father said. "This is the road."

My father is a true man, I thought. It's a duty to be a man. It's like keeping your word. When I grow up, I'll be a true man, too.

Whenever I did something shameful, I said to myself, "How unmanly of you! How could you!" dismayed.

I did not puzzle over his hatred for Aunt Ekavi or that the hatred was returned. It was a natural antipathy, I thought, having no right or wrong. I did not understand the meaning of their insults and had dismissed them from my mind. They were things people say in anger, I thought. People say anything in anger. It was what Aunt Ekavi had said calmly, contemptuously—what had first made my father rile—that stung. "You *would* get a bitch!" she said. She said it the way someone says, "You *would* cheat!" Saying that about my father!

What difference does it make if a dog is a he or a she? People say, "I have a dog." They don't say, "I have a bitch," when they have a she-dog—they say, "It's a she," I thought. They say "life is a bitch," "the weather is a bitch," "son of a bitch," "bitch!" Never "my bitch." Bitch is a curse word.

When we got back to the outpost, I said to Manolis, "Are you telling the soldiers my father got himself a bitch?"

"They got eyes and see."

"They can't see she's a she."

"They see she sure ain't no he."

"Do you say it though—'he got a bitch'?"

"I don't say nothing."

"Do you *think* it?"

"I don't *think* it. She's a bitch."

"How is a bitch different from a male dog?"

"Is woman a man?"

"Animals are the same—male and female."

"Is the ram a sheep? Is the bull a cow? Is the rooster a chicken?"

"Those animals have different heads—male and female. Other animals have the same heads."

"Bigger heads and different look in the eye the males have—those other animals you say."

"How is the look in the eye different?"

"It's different 'cause the soul is different."

"The soul is male or female?"

"Just so."

"Is that why people say, 'Ah, soul of woman . . . '?"

"Yes. They say, 'The woman's soul is a mystery' . . . 'You can't unravel a woman's soul' . . . 'With a woman's soul you won't find the end.' "

"What do they say about the soul of man?"

"They say nothing about the soul of man."

"How come?"

"It's not a mystery the soul of man."

"What is it then?"

"Not a mystery."

What sort of meaning is that—not a mystery? I thought.

"You can read a man's eyes—can read his soul," Manolis said. "Can't read a woman's."

"What about male animals? Can you read their eyes, too?"

He nodded.

I had never stared into a bull's eyes, or a rooster's or a ram's. I went to my mother and asked, "What's written in a bull's eyes, mama?"

"Anger."

"A ram's?"

"Stubbornness."

"A cock's?"

"Conceit."

When you read the eyes, you read the mind, I thought. The male soul must be inside the brain. That's why male heads are bigger. Imagine having your soul in the head! The chest with no soul would feel like a foot then—the whole body, a big, big foot! Awful! My own soul was exactly under the breastbone.

MY MOTHER TOOK to Kyroula the way a little girl, shunning other children, takes to a doll: aloof, immersed in her love, haughty in her joy as though the dog's pranks, enchanting exuberance and frivolous show of affection were a perfor-

mance for her pleasure. Begrudging its charm, taunting it
gently with her foot, she would say, "You're a stupid dog!
Stu-pid! Yes, yes! Stu-pid!" gazing at it with beguiling tenderness. When Kyroula followed her around, for a long time
she pretended not to take notice, then looked down at her
and said, "You fleabag! You shitdog! What do you want,
huh? What, you strumpet? What, you tramp?" in her mocking voice, the warmth and spontaneity, the direct intimacy
one uses addressing one's own. She had never shown till now
this side of her nature. She was an undemonstrative woman,
seeming supercilious in her reserve, living her life in brooding passivity, flaunting her discontent with peevish, sullen
defiance like a child. With us—her husband and children—
her manner had always been as with strangers and people
who courted her affection: cold, formal.

When my father started to train Kyroula, rubbing her
nose in her mess, beating her ruthlessly with a stick, she
tried to stop him.

"If she knows where her food is kept, she knows where to
shit," my father said.

"She's too young."

"We had the children trained by six months. Six weeks for
a dog is equivalent."

He was brutal.

"I've ridden horses that could not be ridden and broken
men who could not be broken. Now a bitch ninny thinks she
can thwart me."

He despised the dog's gentleness, her affectionate nature.
When someone came to the house and she ran to him, jumping with her front paws to their chest, he beat her. When she
wagged her tail at a passerby, he beat her. When we went on
walks and she left his side to run to someone who called her,
he beat her.

She saw the rod raised in his hand and went to him unre-

sisting, tail under haunches, whimpering. Her humility, her
obeisance and penitence for a wrong she did not comprehend
did not appease him.

"Faithless, spineless female," he said. "Hussy!"

My mother looked at him with hatred but did not protest.
Retreating to herself, impassive and resigned, she relin-
quished Kyroula's love without struggle, as she had relin-
quished to him her own life.

She had met my father when she was seventeen, when the
Greek army removed to the Middle East after its defeat to
the Germans and my father was stationed in Egypt. The war
was still going on and people's sentiments heightened. The
Greek community celebrated the officers as heroes. In this
patriotic spirit her father took her—a schoolgirl still—to
her first dance. She saw my father among the other officers
standing with their backs to the band. They were playing a
waltz. He stood motionless, erect, untouched by the tumul-
tuous beauty of the music that was rousing her heart. She
thought, "When he sees me, he'll want to dance. I want to
make him want to dance . . ." They were married three weeks
later, two days after the war ended. They did not know each
other. When she followed him to Greece, she followed a
stranger. She was going to a strange country. The Greece she
had known, her fatherland, spoken of in her home with nos-
talgia and pride, was the Greece of legend, the glorified land
of her schoolbooks. She had had till then an easy, happy life,
sheltered by her father's wealth and affection, an only child.
She had never seen poverty, never done work, never gone out
unchaperoned. She was naive, romantic. The stirring of passion, like stirring life inside her, was the birth of her soul,
she thought. She was reborn. She was seeing the world, the
beauty of the world, for the first time.

On the boat over she said to my father, "We're crossing
the sea to happiness."

My father laughed.

She was bringing with her a trunk, her trousseau of linen sheets hemmed with handmade lace. It was never opened. At the outpost where he took her, the village house where they were quartered was a room with an earth floor and a straw mattress on bare planks of wood. It was her marriage bed, where she awoke.

WHEN I WAS much older my mother said to me of her marriage to my father, "He raped me, he brutalized me. Oh, I don't mean in bed. He was gentle in bed—only place he was gentle. I mean my soul. He raped my soul. I was too young, too ignorant to fight him. I was innocent—innocent, do you understand? I knew nothing of sex, nothing of life—a mere child. I was a good soul, a gentle soul, a *pure* soul, believe me, Anna. I'm telling you, innocent!"

She talked of herself in the past as of another, a person long dead whom she never ceased mourning. Of herself now, in the present tense, she spoke with bitterness and dislike, a cold, leering contempt, as though her usual haughtiness was not for what she was but for the girl she had been—the woman she would have been, had that girl not died defiled inside her. When she said what she thought, what she felt, spitefully, defiantly, like a person with an irredeemable grievance, she said "*I*," "*I*," "*I*" with a vehemence she otherwise lacked, standing up for her dead self—that innocent, gentle, pure girl—as though to avenge her.

Talking of her youth, her face softened, was suffused with light, a tenderness, a joyful pride, as if she were speaking of a lover—the girl Aimilia, not part of her but someone separate, a girl she had loved once, who had died. Her gaze was inward, dreamy, like a man's who has visions, who sees with the heart and what his eyes see seems vile.

This girl Aimilia, from my mother's stories, I got to know and love, too. I longed and grieved for her. I did not believe she was dead. She was in my mother still, living. This sullen, severe, impassive woman, the woman Aimilia, *was* the girl Aimilia, I thought. A person cannot die and live. A person can pretend, can hide. I longed for my mother to come out. I grieved. I loved her. My love for her hurt me.

She said to me, "Do you have dreams over and over—the same dream? All my life—since I got married—even now but rarely now—I dream I'm flying. In my own body, like a bird, without wings, as I am, my body flying, over the earth, in the air, high in the air, light, no weight to it, no weight at all, free. And in my dream I feel, I'm *alive, alive!* I feel happy. Then I wake up, my body heavy with sleep, numb—my heart still flying, my body inside light, happy, as from a drug, the tranquilizers they used to give me or wine. I would think, I want to die like this—now.

"It's the only happiness I've felt—my whole life. Between dreams and waking—a few moments. I used to think, I know happiness. Although only in my dream, I can feel it, can feel it deeper, more strongly than anything else I've felt—completely.

"It's like—it's like hearing music. It floods the soul and you think, No one else hears it but me—it's me and the music—nothing else in the world. And the excitement you feel you recognize. I mean, you don't feel different than yourself, you feel yourself—supremely yourself. You think, This is who I am—this is what I was made for. This! This joy!

"Now that I'm old I dream I *dream* the dream. I think, *in* the dream, I think: I'm dreaming my dream. . . . I don't feel happiness. It's like I'm looking at it. It's like a memory of happiness now—a thought of happiness. I feel nothing—anxiety perhaps. When I wake up, my heart aches—filled with sadness.

"My life is over and I never did fly—never did live.

"I think sometimes—what is life? Why did God make us? Why did God make the flower? The flower in the wilderness—in the forest—the field—the flower that blooms and fades and no one knows it's there?"

AS THE BEATINGS did not succeed in making Kyroula faithful or ferocious, my father locked her in the woodshed, a lean-to without a window, four meters long and one meter wide, and ordered Manolis to feed her bread and water once a day. He wanted to awaken her savage instincts. She was an attack dog, he said. If she didn't know it, she'd learn.

In the beginning she was let out every two or three days. Blinded by the sudden light, her legs staggering from weakness, she crouched toward my father, peeing along the way—incontinent, docile, limply wagging her tail. When he shut her in again, she whimpered, resisting, legs rigid, pushing helplessly on the ground, so he had to drag her. In the end, she was not let out at all.

Her wails, low, long yowls fading in a despair of silence then starting again like moans of anguished, unbearable pain, filled the house night and day. Everyone pretended not to hear. Maritsa hugged her toys, her eyes wide with mistrust and fear. My mother played solitaire, her features immobile and harsh, her eyes hard, staring at the cards on the table, soiled and sloppily laid, the rest of the pack in her hand like loose change. Manolis sat in a corner on the floor, looking down at his boots.

I tried to read. My eyes stayed glued on the same page, the same sentence meaninglessly repeating itself in my head: "The knight's armor was black and was invisible in the dark; only his brandished sword could be seen, glittering in the pale moonlight . . ." I could not go on. When I breathed,

Kyroula's misery got inside me, as though it suffused the air. It stifled me. It made me want to scream. I tried to hold my body inside still, to stop it from breathing. Everything became still then, very still, as in a dream everything seems still. I'm dreaming all this, I thought. My mother, Manolis, Maritsa, Kyroula's cries are in the dream but I'm not in it— I'm dreaming it.

I felt fear, a fear that came and went like Kyroula's cries. When one day no more crying came from the shed, my fear, like the silence, would not end. I paced in the house, terrified.

When my father came home, Manolis said, "I looked in on the bitch. She won't stir, major sir."

He brought Kyroula in his arms and set her down at my father's feet. Kyroula crumbled on her side and lay still. Her eyes were open, glowing with fever. A rattling, raspy sound came from her mouth, a sound like a voice from inside darkness, the sound of death spewing life out.

"You're poisoned with your own venom and want to see everyone else poisoned and destroyed, crawling at your feet," my mother said. "Power! All you want is power. You don't have it, Stephane. You can kill, you can destroy. You killed me. But you don't have power."

"Who has power?"

"Love has power."

"Such as yours?"

"I have no love. I have no self-respect anymore."

"Did you ever?"

"Before you trampled my soul."

"Words."

"Kyroula? Is Kyroula words?"

"You've got the stuff in you or you haven't got it. Men thrown in the hole come out stronger, their spirit fierce."

"Some kill themselves."

"Some are better off dead."

A tear rolled down my mother's face. She wiped it with the side of her hand and, lowering her head, looked at her finger wet from the splattered drop—the small, sole tear, puny weight of the immensity of her sorrow. With her head still bent to avoid looking again at my father, never once having looked at the dog's body between them, she went slowly to her room and closed the door.

My father put his hat on the clothes tree, loosened his tie and went to the living room. He, too, closed the door behind him.

Kyroula was left on the floor in the small corridor. She was breathing more quietly now.

Manolis pulled her body close to the wall and covered her with a picnic blanket.

He picked up Maritsa, held her in one arm and with the other he took my hand. He led us out in the yard.

"The moon's in the sky," he said. "See there? The moon has risen before sunset."

THAT NIGHT I lay in bed awake, my heart crouched shivering inside me, like a panicked animal begging for the blow that will end, with its life, its dread. Fear filled the air, lying in wait, still, surrounding me in the silence, as the silence, in the dark. I kept thinking, Kyroula might die . . . Kyroula might die . . . and the dark became darker, the air black, as the sky was black, black with fear—the shining moon, round and yellow, the eye of fear.

Death is this fear, I thought. This fear outside me, stalking.

With anguish I thought of how I had watched Kyroula suffer at my father's hands without protesting.

I had believed it was wrong to love her. You should only

love what is yours, I had thought. Kyroula was my father's dog. I had no right to protect her. I had no right to love her.

I was wrong. Wrong!

It doesn't matter if you torture someone you love, I thought. It's like you're torturing yourself then—you suffer. But my father did not love Kyroula. He tortured her without love. That is evil. Evil! My father is evil.

If Kyroula dies, he'll be a murderer, I thought.

"Don't make my father a murderer, God dear," I prayed. "Don't let Kyroula die."

But the horror chilled and hardened my heart. My heart did not unbend to pray. I said, "Please, God. Please . . ." but my heart was hard.

God looks down from the sky and sees, I thought. He knows all this. He knows! It is He who made my father— who made the evil in him. It's His doing all this!

"You're mean," I said to God. "I'm saying to You: You are mean!"

I wasn't frightened to say it.

"I hate you," I said to God.

Full of Yourself, powerful, all-too-powerful You are, wallowing in Your might, mean. Be mean! I thought. My love, ungiven, makes of Your power short shrift. *Be* mean!

Suddenly I felt no more fear. I felt nothing—a strange nothing, as though I had no feelings at all, as though I never had had feelings.

"You don't exist for me," I said to God. "Hear me? You don't exist! You think You can do what You want—You can't make me love You! I say, You don't exist!"

I heard the door to my parents' room open and close, then my father's footsteps crossing the hall. He came to a stop, then after a moment, I heard him walk back. Again, the door opened and closed, and there was silence. I was terrified. In my mind, I could still hear the sound of his footsteps thumping, reverberating in my head as though my skull were hollow. I could not evoke his image. I could not feel his presence. Nothing filled out the sound.

IN THE MORNING the place in the corridor where Kyroula had lain was empty. There were no traces of Kyroula left. No one talked about what had happened. No one mentioned her name. Clandestinely, the way Manolis had carried out the dead body in the dark, my parents banished her memory. I felt shut off from them by the uneasy silence, my father's surly, my mother's sullen, Maritsa's scared—the strained denial not just that Kyroula had died but that she had ever existed. They do not feel what I feel, I thought. They're not breathing the air I breathe, still laden with Kyroula's cries. Her life has ended but her suffering lives—will live forever, I thought. Was her soul a light snuffed out, a word, a hollow sound smothered by silence as soon as it was said, "Kyroula," a mere name, all that remained?

Feeling an outcast in my grief, I walked out of the house. I searched the land skirting the village for Kyroula's grave. Everywhere the earth was dry and hard, parched undug crust and loose gray stones. I'll find it, I thought. I'll find it. . . . I walked farther and farther till exhausted I had reached the river. I sat by the bank and cried. What matters a spot? I thought. A grave, unmarked, makes the whole world a grave.

It was a sunny summer day, the air warm and soft, brilliant with light. Light has no feeling, I thought. Darkness feels, darkness holds fear and sorrow—the darkness of night, the darkness of the soul behind the eyes, the darkness of the earth under the ground, fathomless, terrifying. Under the riverbed is darkness, and under the bottom of the well, whose water is cool and clear, and under the wheat that sways in the breeze covering with waving gold the field—

the gnarled roots, like twisted fingers, digging in the earth, a tenacious grip of fear.

I wanted to cry but no tears would come. Grief cooled like steel inside me, a sword of wrath. I had seen life's backside— I had gazed open-eyed in the dark. I knew what was what. My mother had said when you make up your mind whether God exists or not, you're an adult. I'd become adult. The child I was, with Kyroula—Kyroula who was loving, whose downfall was love—had died.

I started back home. I had wandered far away and it was a long walk. It was late afternoon when I got home. My mother was standing by the window anxiously watching the gate.

"Anna! Where have you been? My God!" she said, running out. "Manolis is looking for you. We called the police!"

She dried her eyes.

"The police?"

"Oh! You're all right—all right!"

She hugged me. "You take things too hard—too hard, child."

I broke loose from her arms. She staggered back and looked at me, alarmed.

"Anna?"

I did not answer her. I went to my room and brushed my hair, brushed it and brushed it till it shone, falling down to my waist in lush, glowing waves. I'm myself, I thought. Myself! I stared at the mirror, then suddenly saw behind my reflection my mother's, face drawn, eyes filled with horror.

IN AUGUST, AS every year, we went to my late grandmother's house in her ancestral village, where my grandfather and unmarried aunts spent all summer, the married children, Aunt Vasilia, Aunt Louisa and my father, each having one month.

It was a large, imposing house built like a fortress on a cliff. Small peasant houses, square splashes of white and scalloped splotches of red, sparsely strewn on the slope, were clambering at its feet, a pine forest was above and around it and overhanging the mountain's snowy peak. Its massiveness, decayed grandeur, a stolid ruin, somber, unwelcoming, the house looked abandoned. My two great aunts, Chrysso and Elpiniki, grim ghosts of its past, lived in seclusion inside with shutters shut, dressed in black, starved, scorning my grandfather's allowance to them as charity, letting his money accumulate untouched, moving in the summer, to avoid him, to a small cottage in the plain by fields they owned and rented out to farmers for their meager income. Their rights to the house had been forfeited by their parents in favor of my grandmother, the youngest sister, so she could have a dowry and marry, condemning them to spinsterhood. It was said they had cursed the marriage, that wrong be undone with wrong. My grandmother died young, leaving seven orphaned children.

There were two pictures of my grandmother in the Athens house. The first, taken when she was betrothed, not yet sixteen, shows a young face, frail, delicate, eyes sunken and serene, a diffident smile. In the second, my grandfather at her side, surrounded by her children, she holds Ermioni, the baby, in her arms. Evaggelio and Maro, in pinafores and big bows in their hair, are wedged at each side of her, pushing in her skirt. My father, in a sailor suit, Vasilia, Louisa and Despo, in sleeveless dresses with scooped necks, hip waistlines and short pleated skirts, stand close together, arms at the side. A little apart and to the back stands Ekavi, the only one with curly hair. They all stare at the camera unsmiling, intent. My grandmother looks over their heads, in the distance. It is the same serene gaze as in the other picture, melancholic, enigmatic—the gaze of a young woman thwarted by destiny from her dreams.

In this, her house, hung a painting done a short time before she died. It bore no likeness, yet it was this painting we all thought was she, her beauty idealized, imperial. Her memory, hallowed by death, had become that of a saintly woman; the house where she had lived her childhood sacred, our vacations a pilgrimage.

In this house my father was born, spent the summers of his early childhood, the boy in the sailor suit of the family picture, but for the short-cropped hair, his delicate face indistinguishable from his sisters'. In this house his mother had died, from this house he had followed her hearse, a small boy in short pants still, white starched shirt, his first tie, proud symbol of manhood steeped in mourning black, a boy of eleven told to restrain his sorrow as befits a son. The same day his father said to him, "Now that your mother is dead, you are a man," the heavy, commanding hand on his shoulder ousting him from compassion. It was no longer "the children," but the girls and he, as though in his daughters my grandfather saw the love of his wife surviving, in his son himself, bereft. As though to amend for their mother's loss, he loved the girls doubly. From this love the boy was barred. Also, Ekavi. The boy was a man. Ekavi was not the dead woman's blood.

In both my father's and Aunt Ekavi's aloofness there was an air of belligerence, in their daunting pride the mistrustfulness of someone who has been betrayed. My aunt was irascible, stern, yet not unkind. Roughly, brusquely, sullenly, she showed kindness, as though she thought it futile, her pessimism a new Cassandra's foreboding the meager, prosaic devastation of everyday despair. In her arrogant stature, her intransigence, her dark grave eyes, she looked tragic.

In my father, the hurt became submerged, vengeful, kindled anger. Unlike Aunt Ekavi who had never been loved, had not, after the loss of her own parents other than perfunctorily, been cared for and from as far back as she could remember had found herself on the edge, my father, till his mother's death, had been the favorite child, honored and cherished as the only male. There was inside him a place of gentleness that had once been touched, a place crying out, still tender. It was in his fierceness too fierce, his cruelty too cruel, his hardness too hard, protesting, a rage of denied feeling, lonely anguish. He was an attractive man, compelling, a figure for others larger than life—this heroic image of himself, grand edifice of manhood, as though exacting penance, crushing his life.

My father said to me when I was older, "The slanting glance shows the woman. The staring glance, the man."

He never lowered his eyes.

AS WE REACHED the house my aunts, hearing the car, ran out, my grandfather coming out last and standing at the door silently.

My father said, "Father!"

My grandfather said, "Son!"

They nodded and without embracing smiled while my aunts, exclaiming "Aimilia, you look beautiful! And the children—how they've grown!" rustled us inside, Elengo— come out to take our things from the car—a big suitcase in each hand and a smaller one under one arm, trudging slowly behind us, saying in her husky voice, "Welcome! Welcome!"

In the long trip over, trapped in the car, I felt like a captive being taken to prison. I abhorred this house, reeking of death and piety, hate and misfortune, stifled dreams and spoiled lives. It was not for me, this life. It was not my life. It was my father's life and my grandfather's life, and my aunts' life. I would not live it over again. When my mother took me upstairs to change into fresh clothes and, wetting a comb in a glass of water, braided my hair, pulling it back away from my face, I cried with rage.

Childhood, I thought, was like servitude. A time of indenture. I'll be free yet, I thought. I'll escape. Six more summers, six more years and I'll be eighteen. It will all end then. I'll be me!

At night in my bath, soaking in the warm water, soothing refuge, feeling my body soft and languid, tingling with pleasure, I thought, I *am* me—I *am* me already. How can I wait? Six years! Six years! I thought desperately.

Elengo came into the bathroom wading on heavy feet, shaking my towel in her hand.

"Forgot it, huh?" she said in faked anger. "Old Elengo has no mind but to fetch and carry, huh?"

Seeing me stand up in the tub, the water draining, swirling at my feet, she stopped short, startled, her broad coarse face beaming.

It's me she's looking at like this, I thought. My naked body. Elengo is seeing I'm me—*me!*

She came closer, a strange look in her eyes, a strange smile. She caressed the light curly hair that had started to grow low on my belly.

"Sweet girl, you've grown," she said.

She wrapped me in the towel, lifted me in her arms and carried me to my bedroom.

"But I can still lift you," she said. "I can still lift my baby."

She clasped my body tightly against her breasts and laughed.

In her big, strong arms, I felt big and strong, too, felt as though my body was sinking slowly in her body, dissolving, a sweet serene delight—we were one, Elengo and I. She put me down and I felt small, smaller than I was before, small like a baby, sad and lonely.

She slipped a clean nightie over my head and it fell like a curtain covering my body. Shyly I reached for her hand.

"Elengo, I've been unhappy," I said.

She fluffed my pillow and made me lie down.

"Unhappy? You, my dove? How could you be unhappy, you in youth's blossom?"

"I am."

"Nonsense, child."

"I'll tell you something, Elengo—you alone. When I grow up I'll leave home."

"And where will you go, if you leave home, my dove?"

"I'll go seek my fortune."

"Seek your fortune, my dove? Before you seek your fortune you'll be sought—a face like yours."

"I'll never, never get married."

"Won't you now, my dove? And what will you do if you don't get married?"

"I'll journey in the world."

"Journey in the world! What talk!"

I turned my head away from her.

"My God," she said, "You haven't said your prayers. Don't go to sleep. Get up, child."

"I'm not saying prayers anymore."

"Don't carry on now. Get up and pray."

"I won't."

"God will hear you say you won't."

"So?"

"Anna!"

"If you want to know, I don't like God. I've cut Him."

"This will be on your head, child. Take back the foolish words."

"I never take back my words. *I don't like Him.* He doesn't like me either. We're even."

"God loves you, child. God loves us all."

"He loves *you?* What has he done for you?"

"He's made me, child."

Fat and ugly, I thought. Big, fat and ugly—you who is so kind. But I could not say it. I looked away from her with tears of anger in my eyes.

"Do you love your Elengo, Annio?" she said gently. "Do you love me?"

"I love you."

"Pray for my sake."

For her sake, all the more, I would not pray. God had wronged her, I thought. I cried out loud now.

She took me in her arms. "There, there," she said, rocking me. "God's forgiveness is great—God's love."

She stroked my hair and looked, smiling at my face.

"Would God have made the flowers if He did not love us? Would He have added flowers to this world? Would He have made woman—loveliness?"

She kissed my forehead over and over, saying hush . . . hush.

I nestled my head on her shoulder, sobbing out the sorrow I still had inside for Kyroula. Elengo did not know about Kyroula. Elengo thought I was crying for the love of God.

"God made the earth and the sky," she said. "He filled the sky with the sun and the moon and the stars, and the earth with plants and animals and birds and fishes. Then He made man. Man did not come out beautiful because he was God's first try. So God tried again and He made woman. And God looked at the woman He had made and lo! She was beautiful. And God's hands were happy with love for the woman they had made. And God made flowers with the love of His hands. Flowers are God's love. See?"

"Why is the snake His blessing then?"

"What snake?"

"God's snake."

"God's snake, my dove? Whoever told you such things? There's no God's snake."

But I had seen God's snake! I had seen it. Amidst flowers, amidst His love, I had seen it creeping.

The Man

I REMEMBER OF Tasoula that she wore panties of the same bright-colored fabric as her dresses, with ruffles in the back and lace at the leg gathers, a marvel of beauty to my eyes as I sneaked glances underneath her skirt, bending my knees to peek. She was two years younger than I and, though she could walk, crawled still. She used to play with her toys muttering to herself, a pout of concentration on her small pudgy face, looking solemn and lonely, a spoiled child who screamed for "The Miss" when someone crossed her, pointed an accusing finger and wailed, her eyes darkened with spite.

The Miss had a pale, oval face with hair tied in the back, I think. I don't remember her well. She was young and pretty. I remember the feeling: liking her. I remember my envy of Tasoula because she had a nanny and I did not.

The man had a tight-skinned, deeply lined face as young peasants often have, the lines not a mark of character but of hardship, weathering the face as wind does the land— rugged, toughened terrain, yet with a mouth that was soft, yielding, lips languidly agape. He wore a new suit, stiff from being unworn, tight at the shoulders, badly made. His shirt was open, the collar dirty. He walked slowly, furtively, his muscular body slightly stooped as though shying of its own strength. He had rough, ruddy hands. They were big, his hands.

He came down the street as we were leaving the playground. The Miss and Tasoula walked ahead. I lagged behind. As he came closer to me, he smiled.

He said, "Won't you say hi?"

He knows me, I thought.

"Are you one of my father's soldiers?" I asked him.

"Yes. I've come to see you."

"To see me?"

"Don't you remember how we were friends?"

"Only Anastasis—of all the soldiers—was my friend."

"I *am* Anastasis. Don't you recognize me?"

He took a picture out of his wallet.

"Here," he said. "Take a look at me in uniform."

He did look like Anastasis in the picture—Anastasis, who had been killed in the war, whom I saw in my sleep night after night, his face in the mud, blood oozing from the back of his head, and woke up frightened. Death had changed him totally.

"Anna!" The Miss called. "Do you know this man?" She walked back to us.

"Tell the lady who I am," the man said.

"He's Anastasis," I said. "He's dead."

The man and The Miss laughed.

"I know her father from the army," he said to The Miss. "Go on. I'll bring her home. We'll be right behind."

As we were passing Little Woods, he said to me, "I want to show you a beautiful thing. Over there."

"In Little Woods?"

He smiled.

"What? *What?*"

"Come and you'll see."

We were on the street. Little Woods, to our side, was a small incline of wooded land kept as a park. A dirt path ran across it.

Little Woods is like the mountains, I thought. Like in the war.

We had met in the war, Anastasis and I, up in the mountains where my father had taken me to give me glory. Our neighbor in Athens, Kyra-Lexandra, had said, "Whoever heard of taking a child—a *baby*— to the war?"

"The war's over," my father said. "There are only skirmishes now."

"Stephane Karystine, you are a madman."

My father laughed.

"If I can't give my daughter a dowry," he said, "I'll give her glory."

"I say it again: you are mad."

"So I am."

We traveled in a jeep all day, a convoy. When we reached Mount Grammos, we left the cars behind. The men loaded the supplies on mules. They put me like a pack on a mule, too, side-saddle, riding first, a soldier walking in front pulling the reins, my father on foot by my side. The rest of the men and animals followed single file. Gradually the villages in the valley below got smaller, remote, mere clusters of faint lights. I'm leaving the earth behind, I thought. I'm going to get glory!

I did not know what this thing, glory, was. At first I was excited. Then, as we got higher up, I began to feel afraid. It was as though we were climbing in the sky. The earth down below was a deep hole of darkness. The mountain was all stone, patches of frozen snow in its clefts—a grim, arid landscape. My feet were so cold, I cried. My toes hurt with horrible pain. My father took my boots off and rubbed my feet as he was walking. I cried miserably.

"I want Mama!"

"Daddy's feet hurt, too," my father said. "Everyone's feet are cold. Is anybody else crying? Look at the men!"

"I want Mama! I want Mama!"

"I have a man for you who'll be like your mama."

When we got to the camp, a soldier came out of a tent. "There! See?" my father said. "He's been waiting for you."

It was Anastasis, that man. He took me in his arms and said, "Is this Anna, the Great?"

I nodded. "Are you going to be my mama?"

"Your mama! I'm going to be your adjutant!"

It was cold in the war—very cold and lonely. The men went out in forays and came back late at night. I stayed in the tent with Anastasis. He was the radio man.

He would say to me, "What do you say, chief-ess? Want to go riding?"

He would fall on all fours and I would mount him saying *Gee!* and *Haw!* and he would turn this way and that crawling around the tent and neighing. Or, we would sit side by side on the ground and hold council.

Sometimes we heard the brittle, dry sound of far-off shots, sometimes the explosion of mines. They shook the ground like thunder. I was frightened. Anastasis took me in his arms and calmed me.

"Tough times, huh chief-ess?" he said. "Ah, don't scowl so! It's the way of the war. But it will end. . . . It will end."

"When it ends, I'll have glory."

"Little girl, little girl . . . This is no war of glory," he said sadly. "We're fighting each other. This war has no heroes, only victims."

"What's vic-tims?"

"The men who die in this war."

When he was killed, I said to my father, "Poor Anastasis! He is a victim."

My father for years repeated the story with awe, "There was the tot—three years old—with tears in her eyes telling me, 'Poor Anastasis! He's a *victim*!' "

I said to Anastasis now, "You are a victim!"

He looked at me. "A what?"

He's forgotten he taught me the word, I thought.

"A VICTIM."

"A victim . . ." he said. He smiled. His lips trembled when he smiled. He said, "Come now." He took my hand. His hand was cold and clammy. I felt fear when he took my hand.

The trees were thick in Little Woods, the ground was full of shadows. I didn't want to go deep in the woods. I stopped walking.

"What's wrong?"

"I don't like it that you're dead."

"I'm not dead."

He lowered himself and put my hand on his chest. He had a heartbeat! His heart went *tick tick*. He's a stranger, I thought. A living man! I backed away from him.

"Still frightened?"

"I'm never frightened. I've been in the war! I have glory, if you want to know."

"Come then."

When we came to a small clearing, he said, "Here. Let's sit down."

He took his jacket off and put it on the ground. "So you won't get your little panties dirty," he said. "You don't want to get your little panties dirty."

"You're not Anastasis."

"Yes, I am."

He sat opposite me and opened his legs. "Open your legs, too," he said. "We'll play ball."

He took a pinecone and rolled it from between his legs to mine.

He's not Anastasis, I thought. He's lying. I don't know this man. Yet it was as though I did know him. I felt love and trust for him. It's the woods that's frightening me, I thought. It's the dark. Fear made me want to pee.

I got up. The man got up, too. His face was sad, like someone's who's just stopped sobbing, chest heaving, out of breath still. He hurts, I thought. He hurts inside and he's lonely. He wants to play with me because he's lonely.

"I want to pee."

I started to go behind a bush but he stopped me.

"You pee right here," he said.

He watched me, then opened his pants.

"I want to pee, too," he said.

He took his pee-pee out and squatted.

"I want to pee like you," he said.

He squatted in front of me, his pee-pee hanging out. A drop of blood dripped at its end, bright red.

"Why is your pee-pee bleeding?"

"A little thorn pricked me. Kiss it to make it better."

I shook my head.

"Kiss it," he said. "Kiss it. It hurts."

His pee-pee was not pink and squiggly as the pee-pees of little boys. It was big and dark and thick. I shook my head.

He said, "Kiss it . . . kiss it." He fell on his knees. He swayed back and forth, holding his pee-pee in his hand. He shouted *oooh oooh* in pain, his head thrown back, his arching throat trembling.

He's bewitched, I thought. He's turning into a beast.

His eyes had turned already. They were frightful, glaring.

I started walking backward. If I keep looking at him, he won't come after me, I thought. If I turn my back, he'll give chase. I walked backward slowly. The man stayed on his knees, his head bent low. I'm bad, mean—an awful girl, I thought. The man had begged me to break his spell and I had not done it. He would stay changed now like the king in "Beauty and the Beast," a poor animal, because I had not kissed his pee-pee. It's my fault—my fault! I thought with panic.

I walked backward till he was hid by the trees then

started to run. As I ran, fear ran after me. It gripped my back and dug its claws in. I could feel it clutching my heart. I ran with all my might, frantic. It's only my fear that frightens me, I thought. The beast has stayed where he is. Why am I afraid of my fear? It has no body, fear.

Out on the street, out in the clear, I sat down on the sidewalk trying to get calm. The sun had set. The street was empty. It rolled downhill slithering and swerving. Fear had leapt ahead and was now coming back toward me. I was afraid to go home. I was afraid to stand where I was. I was shaking.

Suddenly a policeman came around the corner, running, and after him The Miss, her hair wild, crying, and behind her our next-door neighbors and "the Stamataki" who sold papers door to door—all of them running, out of breath, calling my name.

The policeman ran past me and into the woods. The rest came to a halt around me. They led me home, walking at a distance, silent.

At our house, my mother stood in the middle of the porch, looking around her as though lost. When she saw us, she started to sob. Standing on the same spot, without moving at all, without covering her face, she sobbed.

OUR HOUSE WAS on the hills, outside Athens. The area had once been farmland and even now on the other side of the hills lived shepherds with flocks of sheep and goats. Gradually what had been country homes became year-round residences with ample gardens. Land was sold off in smaller parcels and villas were built, stately two-story buildings uniform in architecture, with tile roofs and red shutters, vines climbing on the balconies, pines and cypress trees in the yards. On the wide sidewalks the new municipality had planted acacias, eucalyptus trees and rhododendrons. Every few blocks there were small parks, with trees of what had been the old forest left to stand.

Our house was the first house to be built along modern lines, one story, a long rectangle with square windows and rolling blinds, a sore cacophony in the landscape, for years pointed at with derision or alarm—its arid whiteness, bleak harbinger of the style to come. It had been my father's choice of design, a structure as simple and stolid as a barracks building, defying tradition yet conservative in its lack of ornament. It couched our lives in my father's stern, military spirit—conformity that contradicts itself, stiffness which is intransigence, rebellion armored in discipline.

My mother, her delicate, lush beauty, in such a house, like a ruby mounted in iron, a broken young woman, listless, resigned, got up at noon and dragged herself around in house robes all day, unkempt. I was left on my own to come and go as I pleased, a doleful reminder of her husband, this child issued from her inexorably, it seemed, unwanted, unwilled.

Having feared me brutally raped or murdered, she crushed me in her arms. "Mama loves you!" she said, sobbing. "Mama loves you!"

I pulled away, scared. She had never been this way with me.

She took my hand and led me inside. She took me to her room, to her bed.

"Tell Mama what happened," she said. "What did the man do to you?"

"He did nothing."

"You can tell Mama, darling. Don't be afraid of Mama."

"He did nothing."

"Why did you go with him, child? *Why?*"

She took me in her arms, held me tight.

"Did the man touch you?"

"No."

"Did he talk to you?"

"He talked."

"What did he say?"

"He said he would show me a beautiful thing—in Little Woods."

I told her what happened. When I told her about the blood, she said, "Was the blood red?"

"Yes."

"Like—like a nosebleed?"

"It did not *pour,* Mama! It dripped *drop drop.* It came out of his pee-pee hole. Like big red tears, it was."

"You saw it was red?"

"It was blood, I tell you."

She said again, "The blood was red?" She kept saying: "Tell me the truth. I'm your mama. . . . I'm your mama." How could blood not be red? I thought. Why is she telling me she is my mama? I know she is my mama. She made me tell her what happened again and again. I repeated the story, unaltered in detail, even as she pressed me with new questions. If the more she heard it told, the more she began to believe it, the more I told what happened, the more unreal it became to me. I can't tell what's real and what's unreal, I thought. That's why Mama is telling me, "I'm your mama . . . I'm your mama"—so I know she's real.

I said, "I don't want to talk anymore. I want to go to my room."

Mama said: "All right. We won't talk—we won't talk. Stay with Mama though. Stay in Mama's arms—quiet, so."

She had never held me before. My father did not let her. Fondling cripples the fighting spirit in a child—takes out the spunk, he thought. Women did not know how to deal properly with children. "Just look around you," he said. "Nothing but runny-nose brats, spoiled rotten."

If he comes home and sees us like this, he'll kill us, I thought.

When I heard his car, I got off her lap, scared. Even if he doesn't see us, he'll know, I thought.

Mama wasn't frightened. Mama ran to the door and said excited: "They've found her. She's home."

My father ran through the house, came into their room shouting at me, "You . . . you . . . *you*—" in a rage, just as I had feared.

I stood up and bent my head.

"Look at me, you . . . you—" he screamed. "Who told you to talk to strangers?"

He's not angry about Mama, I thought. He's angry about the man. I looked at him, amazed.

"He wasn't a stranger," I said. "He was a soldier."

"Who told you to talk to soldiers? Who told you?"

"Stephane, let her be," my mother said.

"Get out!" he screamed at her. "Get *out!*"

He pushed her out of the room and locked the door.

"Who told you?" he said, slapping me. "Who told you? Answer me! *Answer!*"

How could I say, "You!"? How could I say, "You!" to my father and point?

He threw me on the bed, turned me on my stomach and lashed my back with his belt. I tried not to cry but screams tore open my mouth. I did not understand why I was being punished. I hollered with terror and pain.

After my mother washed the blood off my back, they locked me in my room. I lay on my bed, my body limp, my face sunk in the rumpled sheets, soaking in my tears, dis- tilled sorrow I could taste and feel and say, "It's mine—it's come from me," taking sad solace in this small circle of grief inalienably my own.

I looked at my toys and dolls scattered on the floor. Even Oudi, my dear doll, I saw with dismay. He's filled with straw, I thought. I've been loving a doll filled with straw.

In the middle of the night my mother woke me from a sound sleep and took me out to the hall. Two policemen were there and three MPs with sticks, my father standing in front of them, his arms behind his back, legs open. On a chair pushed against the wall sat the man tied with rope.

"Is this the man?" my father asked.

I nodded.

My father fell on him and beat him with his fists on the chest, the face, the head. The man moaned. He moaned as he had moaned in the woods. He cried, "Mother! Mother mine! Mother! Ah, mother mine!"

I ran to my room, climbed on the bed, crawled to the corner, pulling the sheets to my chin. It's my fault he's being punished, I thought. I gave him away. He'll take revenge. He'll come for me and kill me this time. He doesn't know that I, too, was punished. If only I could go to him! If only I could bare for him my back!

I felt anguish hearing his cries. The bottom of my heart was falling out, I thought—my feelings sinking lower and lower in my belly, writhing, loathsome. I felt nauseous. It sickened me, my body.

FOR YEARS AS a young woman I slept indiscriminately with men, and only just once. I let them have me, unmoved by passion, unfeeling, in my willful passivity frustrating their ardor, making them come slowly, weakly, their sperm impotently dribbling out. Afterward, I asked them, "Do you ever bleed from the penis?"

With a shudder of horror, turning to me a face full of repugnance, they said, "No!" They edged their body away so we no longer touched and shortly sat up, stooping to pick up their clothes. They dressed stealthily, their backs curved with shame. Women feel shame before sex, men afterward, I thought. I did not know what to make of this fact, except to think men deceitful. When they coaxed you to make love, coarse with lust, they swore off shame like a braggart swearing off fear. Later, they lay inert, sodden with sweat, spent, sunk in themselves low as the dregs of their desire. They filled me with contempt. Yet, when I asked a man, "Do you bleed . . . ," it was with inexpiable longing. One day, some man would be truthful, I thought. He would admit to bleeding, to hurting, to shame. I would let him in my body, feeling love. I would let him take me. We'd mix blood inside me. He'd be my brother.

Longing

ONE DAY IN spring, as we were standing in the schoolyard saying the morning prayer, it started to hail. The principal, with a wave of his hand, made the class continue. Hail pelting our heads, we prayed on, our voices raised to heaven like the braying of dogs that God was trying to silence, throwing stones. After the final incantation of "Through the Solicitations of Our Holy Fathers God Have Mercy on Us," we broke ranks and rushed inside like a roused mob, screaming and laughing.

"Mea culpa! Mea culpa!" we hollered with impious hilarity, clutching our heads.

Feeling a wetness in my lap, I put my hand in the pocket of my uniform and found three hailstones. They were opaque white and gleamed like pearls on my palm.

"Look what I have, everybody!" I shouted.

There was sudden silence, a numb sobriety as comes in the wake of hard laughter.

I showed my treasure, smiling proudly. The girls looked at the hailstones, crowding around me, the boys staying their distance till one of them said with a sneer, "Anna's got three stones in her hand. 'Three,' boys! *Three!*"

Earlier that year, explaining the concept of the Holy Trinity, the teacher had said, "The Father, the Son and the Holy Ghost, who proceedeth from the Father and the Son, are three and separate yet one."

She was a thin, jittery woman, a dark birthmark disfiguring the side of her face. The children called her "Two-Tone."

She said, "Dimitri, are you with us? What have I just said?"

"They are separate yet one."

"And what is that?"

Dimitris fidgeted. "It has three parts," he said. "It has three parts . . ."

The children began to titter.

"*What* has three parts? What has three parts that act as one?"

"My prick!" Stratis called out from the back of the class.

The teacher blanched. "Out!" she shrieked. "To the principal's office immediately!"

Stratis strutted slowly out of the classroom.

He was expelled for a week but had made history. A penis was known as "three parts" or just "three" after that.

So now the boys jeered, "Hey, Anna! How about that! Hey, Anna! How does it feel in your hand?"

I closed my fist over the hail. My skin stung, cold and burning. As my eyes filled with mortified tears, the boys relented except for Kostis, who had not laughed at me before but, seeing me cry, fastened his eyes on my face as if he relished my shame. It was a cruel, scornful stare that summoned from the depths of my soul a sudden feeling of love, inexplicable and overwhelming. I stared back at him, stunned.

I kept looking at him during class, my eyes straying uncontrollably, furtive, cowering as he met my glance. My body trembled with strange disquiet, excited and dismayed. The shame I had felt when the boys jeered at me, saying, "Three! Three!" came back to me in hot flashes. Every time I tried to look at him openly, the shame came back and I blushed. His eyes would then fasten on my face again, sullen, hostile.

He was a quiet, solitary boy, frail and sickly, always wearing around his neck a knit scarf. He had soft, plain features, a beauty like a common flower's, forgettable yet endearing as it caught the eye—a delicate, sensitive face, secretive, bespeaking hurt feelings harbored with resentment. He was intelligent, a good student, well-behaved. While other boys boldly provoked punishment, he never gave cause for even a verbal reprimand, yet his good conduct seemed in itself like penance. He sat at his desk with his head bent, eyes lowered as though appeasing his cowardice.

That March, the teacher had chosen Kostis to play The Greek in the skit she put on in class to honor the national holiday. Stratis played The Turk, and Maria, hair loose, long dress and blue taffeta ribbon crossing over her heart from shoulder to waist, played Freedom. The costumes belonged to the school and had been made big for good measure. Staggering from the weight of the stiff, silver-embroidered vest, his hands invisible under the long, flaring sleeves, the skirt of the *foustanella* descending to his feet, Kostis made his entrance—forlorn travesty of Greek rebel—raising instant laughter and jeers. He had to say to Stratis, "Down with you, Mohammedan dog! I defy you, tyrant Turk! Die!" then strike him with his sword and free Maria, standing behind Stratis, rubbing make-believe tears off her eyes. Our role in the play—both chorus and audience—was to cheer, "Long Live Greece!"

They got in place, the teacher gave the signal, we rooted with ill-stifled titters, "Long Live Greece!" and Kostis said, blushing, "Down with you . . ."

"Louder!" the teacher said. "With passion!"

Maria put her hands on her eyes again, Stratis thrust out his chest and glowered, the teacher said, "Go!" and once again we cheered.

Kostis took a wobbly step forward and said, blushing even deeper, "Down with you . . ." His voice, still soft, was now also shaking, making the children howl with laughter.

"Shout it!" the teacher yelled. "What sort of boy are you who can't shout?"

Kostis screeched, "Down, you dog . . ."

"Sit, Turk!" the class mocked. "Heel!"

" 'Down *with* you! *Mohammedan* dog!' Again! And draw your sword as you say, 'Down.' "

Kostis tried to draw his sword, staggered backward and fell. The class regarded him in silence. He sat up, his skirt spreading around him like a girl's party dress and, looking directly at us, sobbed without covering his face.

It was the only time he had done something memorable.

HOW IS IT I like Kostis? I thought. He's a boy! I had begun to hate boys that year. It was not I who had changed, but they. All of a sudden when they looked at a girl, it was no longer in the eye. Their glances slid down her body with insolence, on their face a contemptuous leer. They told dirty jokes, cackling with glee, in their eyes a malicious glint as when they tortured birds. They were vicious and lewd, I thought—loathsome, with their crew cuts and raw faces. If a girl sat a bit with her legs apart, they called out, "I saw your pants," or worse, "I saw your cunt!" When a boy said that to me, I never spoke to him again. I wished him dead. For days and days afterward, I wished him dead. I never forgot an insult.

Once a boy said to my friend Chaydo, "Hey, Chaydo! I saw 'your such!' " Chaydo stared straight back at him and said, "And so? It's not stolen goods! I own it and it's mine."

I admired her immensely.

She was a tall, buxom girl, beautiful and strong, with hair that fell over her face in tangled, reddish brown curls, harsh to the touch like dry grass, and a taut-lipped, large mouth. She had yellow-flecked green eyes, a wide-bridged nose and high cheekbones—sensual, coarse features and an impenetrable gaze, defiant and bitter. She hated boys, too, and stayed aloof from them like myself—unlike the other girls, who brushed them off when they got fresh, affecting anger, only to sidle up to them later and talk, coy and flattered. She and I were best friends.

I asked Chaydo that day after school: "What do you think of Kostis?"

"He's a sissy."

"He's shy, I think."

She shrugged. "Shy/sissy . . ."

"I like him."

"You can't like him! He's 'such a one.' "

"What do you mean 'such a one'?"

"Do you know what men and women do in bed?"

I said I knew.

"Who told you?"

"My cousin Mary, when I was four."

"You *don't* know."

"I do, too, know! The man climbs on top of the woman and rubs his body on her!"

" 'He rubs his body on her . . . ,' " she mimicked my voice. "He puts his prick in her cunt—is what he does."

"I don't believe you! That's disgusting."

"Yes. Disgusting! It's you who likes Kostis not I!"

"What do you mean?"

"Leave me alone. Nothing."

I tried to put my arm around her, but she pushed me away. Whenever I said to Chaydo I liked something, she got angry. Once she stopped speaking to me because I told her I liked the sweet peas in Christina's garden. "Sweet peas are weeds," she said.

"They are not!"

"They are too!"

We screamed at each other, furious. At the end, she said, "So go play with Christina, if you like her sweet peas."

For days she shunned me, courting the friendship of other girls. I looked at her beseechingly, without pride, wanting her back—my love fluttering inside me like a bird beating against its cage when it's first caught. She met my begging glances with disdain, staring straight back at me, as though to say, "The gall you have to think I could love you! You're no one—nothing! You like weeds!"

She's angry at me because I told her I like Kostis, I thought. The terrible things she said are not true. She said them to hurt me.

THE NEXT DAY in math class, the teacher asked Kostis to do a sum on the blackboard. As she called his name, my heart jumped and my body started to shake. I kept my head down, afraid that if I raised it, the whole class would see I was shaking.

"Karystinou!" the teacher said. "Look at the blackboard!"

I looked up, blushing from head to foot. The children laughed. Suddenly everything was as the day before: the children's ridiculing laughter, my feeling of shame, my feeling of love.

When Kostis sat down, I tried to look straight ahead at the teacher, but my eyes kept sliding to the side, in his direction. I put my hand on the side of my face, so I'd stop looking at him.

"Karystinou!" the teacher yelled. "What in God's name is

wrong with you today? Put your arm down, fold your hands and pay attention."

The girls began to look at me with thoughtful, lingering glances, the boys boldly in the eye with affronting smiles. When I went out in the yard at recess, they called out, "Here comes Anna Lovelorn!" They followed me around, saying, "Hey, Side-Glances! Throw us a glance too, and may God save your soul! Deign to look at us or we'll die!" They clutched their hearts and laughed.

Chaydo avoided me. I was alone. Kostis and I were the only children without playmates in the yard. I'll go talk to him, I thought. I'll go tell him, I want to be his friend.

He stood at the side of the yard, near the fence. Behind him, Stratis, Takis and Sotiris were playing marbles. They saw me coming and stopped their game.

I said to Kostis, "Hi!"

"She's *greeting* us, boys!" Stratis said. "Our luck is changing!"

"Nah!" said Sotiris. "She's greeting Kostis."

"Kostis! Make me laugh and I'll cry!"

Kostis hurried away down the yard without looking up.

Stratis, Takis and Sotiris surrounded me, laughing. "Why, hello!" they said. After school, they followed me home, chanting, "Side-Glances! Side-Glances!"

They would come closer and whisper hoarsely, "How about us, Side-Glances? How about it, huh?"

They said, "Side-Glances won't stoop to us because we stink. Do we stink to you, Side-Glances?"

When Kostis passed us, they put their fingers in their mouths and whistled.

"Hey, Beloved!" they yelled at him. "Hey, Beloved!"

Kostis hastened his pace, his shoulders hunched.

"That's right, Kosti," they cried after him. "Run home to your mama or the wolf will get you."

Kostis turned on a side street. The boys kept after me at a short distance. They had stopped taunting me. Their silence was menacing, taut like unvented rage. They'll beat me up, I thought. I started walking faster, my spine rigid, cringing with fear. They did not try to gain on me. All they want is to mock and scare me—to gloat on my shame and fear, I realized. They are vicious. Cowardly. Base. Only a coward mocks. Only a coward insinuates his hate.

I no longer feared them. I loathed them.

At home, I tried to do my homework but, every time I looked at my books, I started to cry. I felt humiliated, enraged. I put my books back in my schoolbag and came out of my room. My eyes were puffy and red.

"What's wrong with your eyes?" my mother said. "You've got pink-eye! What else will you pick up, tyrant? You'll infect us all."

I had had scabies the week before.

I did not tell her I had been crying. What does she care? I thought.

I went to see Chaydo. She lived in the small section of town where the government had built houses for the Asia Minor refugees, little better than hovels, low-ceilinged, huddled close to each other in a common yard. They had no kitchens or bathrooms—only one room where a whole family slept together on floor mattresses. There was a communal outhouse at the end of the yard, a lean-to with a shingle roof and warped door that hung from bent, rusty hinges.

Her father had lost his arm in the war and sat at home all day at a small table in the corner, pouring wine into a water glass with his one hand and drinking it slowly, silently, the lids of his eyes swollen and half-shut.

I called from the door, "Chaydo!"

There was an empty lot overgrown with bramble in back

of the settlement, where Chaydo and I used to go and play. We used to say, "Shall we go 'there'?"

When she came out, I said, "Shall we go there?"

Chaydo did not look at me. "Don't you know when some-one doesn't want you?" she said.

She started walking toward the lot. At least she's talking to me, I thought.

We sat down on our spot.

"Why don't you want me, Chaydo?" I said, crying.

"I want you," she said, looking down. "*Kostis* doesn't want you. Oh, stop crying! Fool!"

"Are we friends again?"

She nodded.

"For ever and ever?"

"For ever and ever."

Kostis doesn't want me and I don't want *him,* I thought, when I was back home. I won't even think about him again. Yet, that night as I lay in bed, his image came to me without my summoning it. I could see him as though he were right in front of me. He was smiling at me. There was love in his eyes. He held out his hand. I took it in mine, trembling with happiness. I had never felt greater happiness.

In the morning, when I woke up, resting my forehead on the cool glass of my window, I looked at the drops of dew glimmering on the grass, their beauty shattering my heart.

It was spring, the air balmy, flowers in bloom. I started for school, happy and excited. Kostis was standing by the gate when I arrived. He saw me coming and his eyes darkened. He did not greet me when I walked by him.

He's pretending to ignore me out of pride, I thought. No hateful glance, no snubbing silence could erase the look of love I'd seen in his eyes the previous night. It had not been a fantasy, I thought. My happiness had been real. My trembling had been real when his hand touched mine. I loved him and he loved me. Still, his shunning me was like the thrust of a knife through my heart.

ONE DAY I was walking with Manolis, when Kostis came down the street from the opposite direction. Manolis said hello to him as he passed us.

"You know him?" I asked Manolis.

"He's the grocer's son."

"Which grocer's?"

"Where we shop."

I knew the store but had never gone in. Manolis did all our shopping for us.

"He works there in the evenings after school."

"He does!" I said, excited.

Manolis looked at me and smiled. "You like him!" he said.

I blushed.

"Why, I believe you're in love!"

He laughed. Even Manolis laughs at my love, I thought. I turned my face away to hide the tears that had come to my eyes.

"Is it like that?" Manolis said kindly. "Ah, Annio! We all go through it when we're young. Eyes that haven't cried haven't loved."

"The boys laugh at me, Manoli."

"Do they now! Laugh back!"

"They call me Side-Glances."

"Side-Glances!" he said, laughing again. "Man-killer, you! Don't you see they like you?"

"They hate me."

"You don't understand boys, Annio. When boys don't like a girl, they leave her alone. They don't even look at her crosswise. When they like a girl . . . when they like a girl at that age . . . I don't know how to explain it to you. Sometimes they feel like bashing her head."

"Why?"

"How should I know why? We don't know what we feel at that age. It's like having a bite that itches—you scratch it till it bleeds. You think you'll make the itching stop but you make the bite a sore."

"How can you like someone and not know what it is you feel?"

"You're too young for me to tell you, Annio. I'll tell you a secret though. No one understands about love, not even the old and wise. There you are, going about your way happy-go-lucky and flop! 'You slip on the melon rind.' You fall flat on your face and that's it—you're in love. It's a tumble, love. A person thinks he's flying and all he's doing is rolling head over arse. Sure other people laugh!"

He sang clutching his heart:

> "Only one I desire and adore
> Her beauty enhances the world
> Holds me spellbound—oh
> Takes my life—oh"

"Only the first love tears the heart, Annio. The rest come and go and the sooner one knows that, the better.

"We're born with love inside our hearts, see. The heart grows bigger, love grows bigger. What happens one day? The body stops growing, the heart stops growing, but love is bigger than man—love still wants to grow. It pushes from inside the heart to burst out and the heart hurts. It's heart-sickness, that. There's no cure for it till a boy meets a girl or a girl a boy, then—*boom!*—the heart breaks open. Love can grow as big as the world."

"Is that why we say 'open-hearted'?"

"That's why."

"Not everyone is open-hearted."

"No. Not everyone meets the right person. Love then shrivels up and dies."

"Are you open-hearted, Manoli?"

He gave me a hug and said, smiling, "I'm open-hearted."

We walked for a while in silence, then I asked, alarmed, "You said love starts to push from inside the heart when the body stops growing?"

"Yes."

I've stopped growing! I thought.

When we got home, I measured myself against my mother.

"Mama," I said. "I'll be short!"

"What new nonsense! You're tall for your age."

"I won't grow anymore."

"Of course you will. You're only eleven. What gave you this strange notion?"

"My heart has broken."

"Your heart has broken. Ah!"

I understood now what had happened when I held the hailstones in my hand: my heart had broken and love burst out! Then, I wondered, Had Kostis' heart broken at that same moment?

I asked my mother, "Mama, let's say, a girl looks at a boy and her heart breaks. Does that mean the boy's heart breaks, too?"

"No, it does not. What's this broken-heart talk suddenly? Only empty-headed girls think about boys at your age. You're a student and your mind should be on your studies. Do you want to grow up and be like other women? I've wasted *my* life, Anna. You're not going to waste yours. You're going to go to the university and learn a profession and become self-supporting. If you want to marry then, it's your choice.

"'A girl looks at a boy and her heart breaks.' Indeed!"

ONCE I KNEW about the store, I started going to the street where it was, standing on the opposite sidewalk, transfixed. Kostis is in there right now! I thought.

It was an ordinary village store on an ordinary village street, with light green, solid wood shutters, closed to keep out the sun's heat. Above the door was a hand-painted sign with the picture of a balance. It said, GROCERY, THE SCALE and with smaller letters underneath, NIKOLAOS KOUTSOGIORGIS, PROPRIETOR.

The road was unpaved. Here and there, tufts of grass and small, solitary flowers sprouted through the hard ground. Low houses, as though squashed by want, stood in a crooked row. The village of Chora sprawled in a valley with uneven, winding streets—the outlying fields, skimpy amidst rocks, its only green. This stark, arid landscape of Macedonia, drenched in the harsh light of the scorching sun, had suddenly become the most beautiful spot on earth for me. As though startled awake from deep sleep, I stared at it enchanted.

General Dimitriadis had said to me when I was small, "Now beauty makes you love and ugliness makes you think. When you grow up ugliness will make you love and beauty, think. That's the kind of person you'll be." But I *see* nothing ugly now that I'm grown! I thought. It felt wonderful to be grown.

I did not wish that Kostis and I would become friends anymore. I did not like to be near him. When we were together in school, my heart beat fast and my throat tightened up. I hated to feel like that. I hoped he would get sick and not come to class. Then I could go stand outside his house and think, "He's in there!"

That was what loving a boy was like, I thought. Wherever he was, you stood outside for hours and whenever you saw him on the street, you followed him. With girls, it was different. With girls, you became friends.

One Sunday afternoon I was standing outside Kostis' house, when his mother came out in the garden and sat on a stool by the well. She took a small ball of yarn from her apron and started to crochet. Kostis must be still taking a nap, I thought. The shutters of the house were closed. A little later, he came out, too, and stood sleepily at the door. Without looking up from her work, the mother said, "You've awakened, my sweet? Come sit next to me, my life!"

Kostis walked over to her, rubbing his eyes, and sat on the ground by her feet, resting his head on her lap. She gave him a quick, loving glance and went on crocheting.

If only she were my mother! I thought.

Later, when I was with Chaydo and she and I were playing in our lot, I asked her if she had ever wanted a brother. She said no.

"I never used to before but—suddenly—this year, I started wishing I had one," I said.

"What for?"

"So I'd be proud of him. He'd do all the things I can't do because I'm a girl, and I'd be proud of him."

"What things?"

"He'd beat up all the boys who look at me you-know-how and follow me around. He'd beat them up—that's the first thing. No boy would dare even come near me because of him."

"Some brother!"

"I don't know why you laugh!"

"What else would this brother do—other than beat other boys?"

"I don't know—heroic things."

"Such as?"

"I don't know, I tell you. Heroic things! He'd be noble and fearless. He'd die for Greece."

"May he rest in peace."

"I'm serious. Sometimes, I think I do have a brother. Sometimes, I believe I'm not my parents' child. I think I was born with a twin brother and my parents stole me and left my brother with my real mother. One day, we'll meet."

Chaydo chewed on a blade of grass. "Ugh! It's bitter!" she said.

We stole a plank from the shack they were building at the end of the lot and put it on a barrel to make a see-saw. As we went up and down, a keen, thrilling pleasure shot through my body, as when my father drove the car and we went over a bump.

"We'll fall off!" I screamed, laughing. "Stop! Stop!"

Chaydo, instead of stopping, bounced on her end of the plank harder and harder, throwing her head back and shouting, "One in the air, two on the ground! One in the air, two on the ground—I'll never come down!"

When we got off, our faces flushed, out of breath, I said, "Did you feel funny down there?"

"Did you?"

"Yes."

We started to giggle. As soon as we'd manage to pull a straight face, we'd look at each other and laugh again.

"You are silly!"

"*You* are silly!"

"We have to look at each other and try not to lower our eyes," she said. "That will cure it."

We stood face to face, raised our eyes, and bent over laughing again, our foreheads touching, locked like two rams.

That night in bed, I touched myself with my hand. My

fingers fit in, snug and moist as though I had put them in my mouth. I stroked myself, and the same pleasure as on the see-saw spread in waves through my body and choked in my throat. I let out a cry. Had it gone up more, it would have unseated my mind. I was horrified. It was as though inside my body was trapped another body. It was not me, this other, pleasure-feeling body. It was like something had crept stealthily up inside me, aiming to take me over. I was on to it. And yet, the pleasure was so wonderfully keen, I was hard put to resist.

Every night before going to sleep and in the morning when I woke up, I stroked myself between the legs, under-hand, shy, shameful as though I were touching a stranger I scorned but could not shun.

A FLAT, BARE expanse of land stretched in front of our house. At the far end was a marsh, with clumps of gorse and reeds growing in the shallows. It was a bleak view, as though our house were looking out unto the edge of the world. One morning, I woke up and saw tents being set up, a large encampment, rising in the shimmering heat like a mirage. There was going to be a fair, my parents told me. They pointed to a Ferris wheel and a boat swing being assembled from what had seemed a pile of scrap metal.

After they set up their tents and stands, magicians, acro-bats, giants and dwarfs, fortune-tellers, peddlers, sat on the ground in groups, playing cards, or by themselves, legs stretched out, eyes fastened on scuffed, dusty shoes, sipping wine. Their clothes were torn and worn, their faces sallow, their eyes like those of beggars squatting on the wayside too weary to stretch out a hand.

"The spectacle!" my father said. "Able-bodied men, think-ing themselves too good for honest work."

He refused to give me money to go.

I asked if I could use my own allowance.

"Your money is yours," he said. "You want to pay to be made a fool of, go ahead. It's all tricks—you've been warned."

I said, I *would* go all the same. I thought my father would be angry but he smiled.

"You're raising your own flag, Anna?" he said. "We all have to fight our battles, I guess. Truth is better learned when it wounds us."

"May I have my allowance for next month, too? Chaydo would like to go, too, I'm sure, and her parents don't have money."

"I'll give you money for Chaydo. It doesn't have to come from your own. I'm glad to see you're generous," he said. "One should always be generous with friends. A generous man is a brave man. I never knew a brave man who was tight-fisted."

I'm generous and brave and I'm going to the fair! I thought, excited. I ran to Chaydo's and said, "I got money for us to go to the fair tonight."

"I can't go," she said. "I've got nothing to wear."

"Wear your blue dress."

"It's gotten too short."

"You wore it last Sunday."

"I've grown since last Sunday."

"You *have* not!"

"I have, too!"

"Come as you are."

Chaydo agreed to go in her old dress, as though she were doing me a favor. She was grumpy. On the way, she kept kicking stones with her feet. "This dress is too short, too," she said. "I hate fairs!"

She watched the magic acts, scowling with skepticism. Like my father, she said, "It's tricks."

"If it's tricks, how is it done?"

"I don't know how it's done. I know it's tricks."

We passed a tent with a placard in front of it, showing a girl our age in a bikini. Chaydo said with a smirk, "Shameless hussy!"

"She's from Athens! Girls in Athens dress in bikinis all the time. You're a hick!"

"Girls from Athens are hussies."

A short man in a black suit and bowler hat stood next to the placard, calling out, "Come ye! Come ye! Gentlemen young and old, sneak away from your wives. See Mirabella, the Girl Siren, the Child Femme Fatale—a pleasure to last your lives!"

Some kids from school beckoned us over.

"There's a hole in the tent—in the back," they said.

There was a line, each child waiting impatiently to peek.

"What does she do?"

"Nothing."

"How—nothing?"

"Nothing! She dances. Look!"

A woman stood on a small platform. She played the accordion and sang:

> "I'm in a bind, God, I find
> I love Kiki but it's Roro I desire
> I'm in a bind, God, what to do
> I love Kiki—I want Ro"

The girl of the placard danced in front of her, swiveling her skirt right and left, raising it with her hands as she kicked her legs.

"She must be doing something we can't see from the back," Maraki said. "Folks have gone to see the show two and three times."

"Let's go find out," Chaydo said.

"Only men are going in," I said. "Women aren't allowed."

"Says who?"

"Can't you see?"

"Is it written?" She started to push her way through the crowd.

"Chaydo, they won't let us in!"

"If you have money, they let you in and if you don't have money, they don't—same as anyplace else. You pay, you get. You pay a little extra, you get a bow as well," she said.

She took the money from my hand and gave it to the man. He let us pass.

"She's so pretty!" I said, looking at the girl.

"She's painted up."

"So what?"

"So, she's a hussy."

We moved away from each other, angry.

The girl had dark, sunken eyes lined with kohl, and platinum hair that fell to her shoulders in glowing waves. It was dark in the tent except for the spotlight above her head. It fell over her like a shower of gold dust. If she moves out of the light, her beauty will vanish, I thought. Such beauty can't be real. It was the magic of magic!

When we got out, the children asked what we saw.

"She shows her pants—is what she does," Chaydo said.

I saw a fairy in the girl, she saw a strumpet, I thought.

"We don't believe you!" the children said.

"Tell them if I'm lying, Anna," Chaydo said to me.

I bent my head.

"Tell them!" she said. "Tell them!"

I walked away from her.

"Judas!" she said, running after me. "Judas! Why did you let them think I'm lying?"

"They were not her pants. They were her uniform! They had sequins on them."

"She bared her ass for the men to see! They were gawking at the sequins, were they!"

"Go away!"

"You're not telling *me* to go away! *I'm* leaving *you!* I never want to speak to you again."

I said nothing. She said, "I never liked you one bit."

"Neither did I."

"I hate you!"

"And *I* hate *you!*"

"Well, good-bye."

"Good-bye."

I went back home and sat on our porch. The fair stretched out in front of our garden, its colored lights glimmering in the night, music and noise from the milling crowds filling the air. It was as though our house were a ship, docked at a strange harbor after sailing on a boundless, empty sea.

Manolis came out and stood next to me, leaning on the rail.

"So, what did you see at the fair?" he said.

"Samson, the Giant. He had long hair and wore a loin-cloth and bent bars of steel. . . . Olaf, the Unsurpassed. He sawed a woman in half and put her back together without a scar. . . . The Man Who Defies Gravity. He rode a motorcycle inside a barrel, round and round all the way to the top and did not fall. . . . And . . . Mirabella, the Girl Siren. She's the most beautiful girl in the world."

"Ah, land of dreams . . ." he said.

It's not the fair that's full of dreams, I thought. It's life. At the fair, you see what you see—beauty, magic. It's life that's full of dreams—that the world is beautiful, that we love, that we are happy.

I thought of Chaydo, I thought of Kostis, and felt sick. What a fool I've been this year! I thought. What a fool!

.   .   .

DURING THE TIME the fair stayed in town, I went every evening down to the garden, stood behind our fence, arms stretched out on the mesh wire, and watched the lights come on, sad with longing.

What am I longing for? I thought.

One day, as suddenly as it had come, the fair moved away. They dismantled the tents, put them on trucks, and drove away in convoy. The field in front of our house was again barren, flat land stretching to the marsh.

At sunset, the men of the regiment's cavalry division brought out their horses to exercise them. They galloped in formation—their hooves' clattering, a joyous thundering of glory. Behind them rose a cloud of dust.

Love

MY MOTHER'S PARENTS had moved to Athens in the early fifties, leaving Egypt when Nasser began to nationalize private business. Many Greeks started coming back then, flaunting their wealth and acquired European culture in a country recently put through a ravaging occupation by the Germans, a civil war involving the Americans and the British, a nation left poor, resentful of foreigners and now of these Greeks, foreign in their spirit. They became a community apart, distinguished from the native Greeks by the term "Egyptiates"—to them a name of distinction, to others a label of scorn. They were thought successful through easy circumstances in a colonial system, their achievement discounted, their European manners mocked.

My grandfather had retired forcibly. With the takeover by the Egyptian government, his business went bankrupt. He was a ruined man, his dignity effaced. Others, anticipating the political change, had pulled out their money in time. My grandfather, with staunch fatalism, stayed on—an act of futile nobility that years of poverty in his later life did not make him disclaim.

Every day, he dressed formally in a three-piece suit to read the morning paper, changed to old clothes to work in the garden, and dressed up again to read the evening paper— even in print the world requiring, he believed, one's prim attention. He had dinner sitting at the head of the long dining-room table across from my grandmother—between them, four chairs on each side and unbroken silence. As though food were his last tenacious grip on life, he ate with somber gluttony, his eyes joyless, avid. Afterward, he sat in the drawing room, always in the same chair, his legs stretched out and crossed at the ankles. Entrenched in the relics of his old home—massive ornate furniture, velour curtains with tassels, brocade upholstery with gold fringes and dark carpets—he smoked for hours, sullenly contemplating his decline.

He was a tall, narrow-shouldered man, his body—taut with a testiness at odds with his frail frame—rigidly erect, a rod of respectability and reserve. He was fair, with pale pink skin and thinning, graying blond hair, light blue eyes reddish at the rims. He was too shy to be overbearing, yet appeared supercilious, guarded with mistrust, a man not likable at first sight. He had a sensitive nature, shamefully bared in rare outbursts of feeling, but on the whole acted meticulously from a strict sense of duty, holding himself remote, sheltered in self-righteousness like a proud virgin—his unbending moralism, conservative and respectful of tradition though it was, giving him an air of eccentricity.

He had married in his forties a woman twenty-five years younger. He was sensually squeamish but had deep affection for his wife, tolerance and tenderness for her youth. It was a happy marriage—for him, so guarded and solitary a man, because all he expected was the tranquility of trust; for her, because she had the temperament of a meek child, its easily contented nature. There was between them the intimacy of shared silence—in him reserve, in her resignation—the instinctive bond of society's misfits. If he never used endearments, his affection was held whole in his pronouncement of her name, Ismini, the word in his voice beautiful and gentle, trailing softly at the end of a sentence. She, diffident, uncontentious, obeyed his wishes, embraced his views, cherished his cranky spirit.

She had been born to her mother late, in the untroubled years in a woman's life when a child brings unhoped-for joy, evokes a love beneficent and gentle as parents feel for their young when their personal ambition is ebbing. She was the youngest of eight children already grown—some of them out in the world or married—cast in the margin of their lives. She looked up to them with a feeling of inadequacy she retained her whole life. The bloom of her youth, like the glimmer of a sole star in the desolate dark, shone on her aging parents, their last lasting happiness. She was loved with a love that asked for nothing back. In a baby picture of hers I own, she nestles in her mother's arms impassive, her eyes blissful, limpid with trust.

She grew into a short, plump woman, her body alluring in its yielding softness, a radiant femininity, as though overflowing, suffusing her rich flesh, the fat like a layer of ebullience. She had a lithe walk, despite her weight, light and graceful on her feet. Her face was round, beautiful, had a guileless expression that changed to incredulity or wonder, joy or sadness, transparent to emotion like a child's. When she laughed, her body rippled with unguarded pleasure. When she smiled, her cheeks furrowed with dimples, her eyes narrowed almost shut.

In Egypt she had had a housekeeper and servants. Here, with the loss of my grandfather's fortune, she took over the housework like a novice bride, proud and eager. He did the errands and shopping, she the cooking and cleaning. Unused to the tasks, overintent, they were, in their old age, like children playing house. In the evening, she dressed for him in her old "good" dresses, years ago gone out of fashion, faded and stretched from wear, frayed relics of elegance, sad outlines of spent beauty.

.   .   .

WHEN I WAS six years old, my father was stationed near the Bulgarian border. The closest school was accessible through steep mountain trails, an hour away by mule. It had one teacher, one classroom, and most of the children spoke Slavic. It was decided I should live with my mother's parents in Athens and go to a proper school.

Leaving me in their home, my mother said to reassure me, "You'll love your grandma, you'll see." It was a promise, I thought, as when she said when I was scared of the dark at night, "Close your eyes and sleep. When you open them, it will be light." When I open my eyes in the morning, I'll feel love for Grandma, I thought. It would happen like a miracle—love would come the way light came.

The house was newly built, with low-ceilinged, square rooms in the practical, sparse, postwar style when houses were built cheaply and quickly with little eye to appearance. Inside, the old furniture—ornate, stately pieces crammed close together, grotesquely at odds with the rooms' small space—loomed darkly as doom, the past's unwieldy nemesis, history that cannot be transplanted. For me, however, a child still—the world of fairy tales and the world outside me mingling in my mind indistinguishably—solemnity in things had a magical enchantment. Gloom held the secret of powers unseen. The house enthralled me.

As soon as my mother was gone, I went from room to room, like a new kitten, sneaking in corners and behind furniture, crouching excited to look underneath. My grandfather, sitting in his chair, his shoes freshly shined, his starched collar pressing his neck, watched me with amusement, his eyes enlarged behind horn-rimmed glasses. The legs of his chair had paws with curled claws. I looked at the other pieces of furniture in the room. They all had paws! I was thrilled beyond words.

On the end tables by the sofa were bronze statues—full-bodied and not just busts as in my other grandpa's house. Grandpa Damien had busts of Plato and Aristotle in his study. These statues were of men from a foreign land wearing tights and shirts with flounces and floppy hats.

"Are these men foreign philosophers, Grandpa Zisi?"

"They are nobodies."

"Why do you have statues of nobodies?"

"Because they are beautiful."

One statue was of a little boy pulling up the hem of his shorts and looking at his birdie, ready to pee.

"Why do you have that?"

"It's well done. The pose is natural."

"We should turn him around to face the wall." That would make it more natural, I thought.

Grandpa laughed and said, "The little boy is a work of art, Anna."

Peeing, in that case, had deep significance, I thought. I looked at the little boy, abashed. No matter what a thing was, if it was art, it had deep significance—even a small chipped shard from a broken pot. It was put in a case and people lined up to see it, opening their eyes wide. My other grandpa took me to the National Archeological Museum every time my parents brought me to Athens. "A child should be exposed to art early," he said. "A child's taste should be cultivated and trained." He pointed at broken marble statues and said severely, "Look at this!" and "Look at that!" the way he pointed to my mistakes when he taught me spelling. It was because the statues had parts missing and deformed, I thought.

I had not seen a correct work of art till now.

I sat on the armrest of Grandpa's chair but he said I should go sit on the sofa. "Go sit on the sofa where you'll be more comfortable," he said. "You don't want to break this chair. That's right. Sit down and talk to me. Tell me about yourself."

"No, no!" Grandma yelled from the kitchen. "I want to hear, too. Wait till I come."

She came in the room huffing and puffing. She wore, clinging to her body shiny and slinky, a yellow print dress with small little flowers. It had a lace collar on top with bouncing pearl buttons going down in a row between her breasts.

"Can you believe she's starting school?" she said. "Look at her!"

Grandpa shook his head.

"Come!" Grandma said. "Come give me a hug! Do you remember your grandma? Do you remember when you came to Egypt?"

"I remember the elephants."

"And your grandma?"

"No."

"You remember the elephants and you don't remember Grandma! And I who cried and cried when you left!"

"She was eighteen months, Ismini."

"Ah! She doesn't love me."

"Of course, she loves you!"

"Won't she give Grandma a hug then? I want a hug."

I went up to her and hugged her.

"Oooh!" she said. "Now a kiss! Oooh! What a sweet kiss!"

At night, when it was time to go to sleep, she took me to the bed she and Grandpa shared. Grandpa would use my room, she said, just this once, because it was my first night.

We lay side by side, the sheet rolled down at our feet. I had not slept with anyone on the same bed before. People have the same dream when they sleep together, I thought. What if I sleep first? I watched Grandma anxiously. She had closed her eyes.

"Grandma, I'm awake still."

"Close your eyes and you'll sleep."

I closed my eyes.

"I'm awake still."

Grandma laughed. She put her arm under me and pulled me close. "Try again," she said.

I turned on my side, put my head in the crook of her arm, my face on her breast.

"Grandma, how nice you smell!"

"You like my perfume, little heart?"

"I like it. And I like your belly, Grandma. It's like a balloon your belly."

I touched it with my hand. It was soft and squishy and it moved *pluff pluff.* I climbed on top of her, my body rolling on her big belly, my arms flaying for balance.

"I'm swimming on you, Grandma!"

Grandma laughed. She pulled me up to her face and kissed me. We hugged tight. I pressed my hands to the top of her bare arms, then lifted them to put them lower and lower down, the coolness of her soft, smooth skin against my hot palms giving me a startling pleasure.

"I'll make you hot, Grandma! I'll make you hot like me."

When I got down to her wrists, she clasped my hands.

"I have you," she said. "You can't move."

We wrestled and Grandma won.

"Now lie quiet and go to sleep."

"You won't go to sleep without me?"

"I won't go to sleep without you."

But Grandma slept first and I lay awake a long time. When in the end I slept, I had my own dream, alone and lonely.

When I woke up, it was morning, the air dark amber from the filtering sun. The mirror on the armoire reflected the edge of the bed and a chest of drawers with a big basin on it. I could not see myself. I was frightened and lonely—lonely as in my dream.

Grandma's place on the bed was empty. She had vanished. I got up and opened the door. The corridor was dark and empty. There was complete silence. A smell of closure and mould hung in the air. I walked through the corridor and small hall to the dining room, the drawing room, the study. Everywhere the blinds were drawn and there was no one in sight. I was very frightened. I screamed in panic, "Grandma! Grandma!" and started to cry.

My grandmother came running from the kitchen porch.

I looked at her, the fat, laughing woman who had taken me in her arms the night before, and she now seemed like a stranger. Mama lied to me, I thought. It was morning but I felt no love for Grandma. Covering my face with my hands, I sobbed. My parents had abandoned me, I thought. I was alone in the world.

Grandma took me in her arms and stroked me and I began to feel better. No one had held me when I cried till now. My sorrow is sinking inside Grandma, I thought. That's why I feel better. She's taking my sorrow inside her, a part of my soul. Grandma had a part of my soul inside her! No one had a part of my soul inside them before. No one had wanted my soul before.

LOVE WAS AN untenable longing, I had thought. Love was something only I could feel. Now, when my grandmother's eyes rested on me, gentle and kind, their soft light shining deep through my heart, her face, just for looking at me, beaming with delight, I knew she, too, felt love. Grandma and I were alike, I thought. Grandma and I felt love.

I grasped her in my arms, cuddling my head in her lap. My arms could not reach all the way around her. As she was bigger, her love was bigger, I thought. I only had as much of her love as I could hold. She had all of mine—she could hold me all. She has love left over—she loves Grandpa, too, I thought. I felt jealous of Grandpa. I did not want them to be alone. I stayed close to Grandma, watching her like a hawk.

Wherever she went, I followed. Everything Grandma did was serious, I thought. Her face frowned in concentration as she moved here and there, her slippers flapping on her feet, going *clack clack clack,* busy and self-important.

"What are we going to do now, Grandma?"

"We'll sweep the floor."

"What are we going to do now?"

"We'll shell peas."

Whatever the task, whether following at her heels or sitting next to her on a chair, elbows on knees and my head gravely in my hands, Grandma and I did it together. I watched, transfixed, as she nodded her head to the music from the radio while she darned a sock, her short black hair bouncing, thick and curly, her eyes downcast, dreamy with thought, fingers agile and soft thrusting the needle in and out of the cloth.

She wore a dress of shiny blue rayon with white dots that opened in the front like a shirt showing her cleavage, a shadowy dimple like the corner of a secret smile. Her heart was smiling, I thought. Grandma had a smile in her body! Her body was always pleased. Grandpa's body was solemn and long. It was not happy and fat, Grandpa's body. When he took me in his lap, I felt his bones. I did not like Grandpa's body.

When it was time to go to bed, I wanted to sleep with Grandma again. Grandma said no. My grandfather said,

"It's been a traumatic experience for the child—suddenly being left alone. Let her."

I said to Grandma, kissing her, when we were in bed, "I want to sleep with you always—always!"

Grandma laughed.

"Anna loves you, Grandma."

"Grandma loves you, too, little heart."

I was afraid to sleep. I would be alone in my sleep again, I thought, far away from Grandma.

"Grandma, I want you to be in my sleep. Please be in my sleep!"

Grandma said if I thought of her hard before closing my eyes, she'd be in my dream. I had no dream at all that night, however, and every night after that I had no dream.

I was terrified to sleep. I became dead at night, I thought. In the morning I woke up from death. If Grandma was not there to wake me, I would stay dead. The only reason I came back to life was because Grandma woke me.

I had paroxysms of crying when they tried to put me to bed in my room.

"I'll die if I sleep there," I said. "I'll die!"

Finally my grandfather moved permanently to my room. He put down the siderails of my bed and slept crunched up till the new bed came.

Even so, there were the three hours, between nine sharp when I was put to bed and about midnight when my grandmother came to sleep, when I still thought I'd die. I waited for her, fighting off the silent, fearsome darkness. To fall asleep would be to surrender to the dark, I thought—to the endless night from which there was no waking. When I began to feel drowsy, I sat up in bed in panic. The dark was gaining on me—closing in. I had to *think—think* to keep away. I had to make sure Grandma came to lie next to me before I fell asleep. What if sleep overcame me? I was terrified.

When at last Grandma came, she said, "Still awake, little heart? Are you a vampire perchance and haven't told me?"

I clasped her in my arms.

"Oh, my grandma! My grandma! I thought you'd never come. I thought you left the house."

"Left to go where at such an hour?"

"I don't know. I thought you left."

I curled in the hollow of her waist, my head under her arm, and let myself fall asleep at ease. Grandma would not let me die. Her love would brave the dark night and call me back from the death of sleep. Tomorrow I would be alive again because Grandma loved me.

THE INERTIA OF my grandparents' lives, carried on as though their fate had been lived out, was stifling. I was idle. Daydreams filled my time—fantasies that I thought were real, as I believed that what was read to me was real. If my nights were wakeful with terror till sinking, dreamless, to sleep, my days floated on dreams, blissful. I was the heroine of adventures—Anna, the greatest child of all. I did wonderful, magic-wrought things, if only in my mind. I was like people in books, I thought. Other people were not like people in books. Around them, I had to pretend my life was dull like theirs. I lied. Only to my grandma I told the truth. I told my grandma all my imaginings.

"What things—what marvels you relate!" she said.

Grandma was proud of me for slaying dragons and going to feasts with Ali Baba and the forty thieves.

I already knew how to read and write. I knew arithmetic, too. Grandpa Damien had taught me. I did not understand why I had to go to school. "You have to go to school to become an educated being," my grandmother explained. It was not clear to me what an "educated being" was. I dreaded to become it, not knowing what it might be. I did not connect education with learning but saw it as the incalculable result of days-long sitting in the same spot with hands clasped, fingers entwined, and feet flat on the floor.

During breaks the children laughed and played. I watched

from a distance. I did not know their games. I stayed solitary. When in time I got to know some of them, I did not make friends. I had my grandma. Grandma was my friend. Children were friends with each other because they did not have a grandma. They lived with their mama and papa. When they asked me where my own mama was, I said I did not have a mama. I was miraculously born.

When I got home, Grandma waited for me outside the door. When she saw me, she opened her arms wide. I ran to her and she hugged me. "What happened in school today?" she asked.

"My good fairy came to class. The children saw my good fairy and they turned to stone. The teacher turned to stone, too. My good fairy said, 'Annoula, do you want to stay with these stone children or do you want to be with me?' 'I want to be with you,' I said. A big white cloud came down from the sky. My good fairy said, 'Annoula, get on the cloud.' I got on the big cloud and my good fairy got on the big cloud, too, and the big cloud lifted up up, up in the sky, and the sky was red and yellow and green and all colors and a ship came floating by and there were pirates in the ship with swords and the pirates said, 'Who's there?'

" 'Advance and be recognized,' the pirates said."

I left my story hanging there. I was never able to finish my stories.

In the evening Grandma read what Grandpa Zisis mockingly said were cheap romances. She smiled to herself or frowned, excitedly skipping ahead to find out what happened. I sat at her feet and nudged her, twisted between her legs, pulled at her sleeve, to no avail. Grandma read and read.

"Quit being a pest," she said.

Grandma liked soap operas, too, and listened to the radio when they came on, sitting close to the console, dropping whatever she was doing in midcourse and running to the living room exclaiming, "*The Concierge* is on! *The Concierge* is on!" Grandpa pooh-poohed her low taste but, behind his newspaper, eavesdropped, delivering comments on the plot— a one-man sarcastic chorus.

She let me help her fold the sheets when she took them down from the clothesline, she pulling at one end and I at the other like a tug-rope, then walking slowly toward each other, the sheet held in raised arms, to fold the ends together. When we pulled, she said, "Op! Op! With all your might now!" When we walked back to each other, the raised sheet blocking our view, she bumped into me crying, "Collision! Stop!" and I bent over laughing, dropping the sheet on the ground, and Grandma had to dust it.

Every time she did the wash, she called down to the garden from the window, "Anna! The wringer!" and I ran upstairs two steps at a time to watch the clothes go through the wringer with rapt absorption.

On Fridays, when we fasted, to make me finish my soup, she told me that the iron of the lentils, like a magic potion, would make me undefeatably strong.

"Like Hercules?"

"Like Hercules!"

I drank my soup to the last drop.

"Now, come fight me and see who wins," Grandma said.

She let me pummel her with my fists and collapsed panting against the wall. "What did I tell you?" she said.

When she started to knit something new, she put the sheaf of wool yarn around my hands and pulled at the end of the thread to wind the ball. I stood with forearms raised, the thread unfolding from me to her—the soft, bright-colored yarn of our love.

At night she read to me from the books my mother had had as a child—that they had saved and brought back from

Egypt—patiently, for hours, with each character changing her voice. I listened cuddled next to her, my head on her arm, asking again and again the meaning of words. Grandpa, who followed the story from the other end of the room, explained in his grave, peremptory voice, preempting the right to instruct me.

I disliked Grandpa. I did not want him to teach me. I wanted my grandma to tell me what things meant. His gentleness and kindness to me—the beseeching tenderness under his severe mien—had no effect. I felt low-down and grouchy to hate him, yet my heart was closed to him, filled with spite.

Grandma would ask, "How much do you love me?" She would put her palms together, pull them apart a little and say, "This much?"

"More."

It was a game we played often. She would open her hands wider and wider, and keep asking, "This much? This much?" and I said, "More! More!" till her arms were open wide, stretched out at her side.

"More!"

"How much then?"

"From here to the sky!"

Grandma would kiss me and laugh and Grandpa would look at us and laugh, too. I would stare at him sullenly and, with the vicious cruelty of a child, turn my back.

MY GRANDMOTHER SAID to me when I was older, "When my father had a stroke I went to live with him. Our houses were close and I would go cook for your grandpa, then go back to my family home. We had a full-time nurse and she and I would sit by my father's bed and knit. He could not move one side of his body at all and he could not talk. The nurse—

God bless her soul, she's dead now—said to me, 'It's good to talk to them—they can hear.' So I talked to him. I talked to him all day long. He used to like to read the paper, so I read the paper—you know me, I never read the paper—and then told him all that was in it. That took one, two hours. What could I say to him after that? I told him what I had cooked that day—the recipe step by step, you know—what flowers had bloomed in the garden, what the dog had done. Whatever happened in my life—I told him. But what ever happened in my life? For the first time I thought, What a boring life I've got! How unimportant! So insignificantly have I lived that the story of my life is boring my own dying father.

"This was during the war, when they were bombing Cairo. The sirens would blow, and it was impossible to move him. The doctors had said he was dying and all the children had come to be with him. They said to me, 'Leave him! Go to the bomb shelter. He's dying anyway.'

"How could I leave my father?

" 'What can you do for him?' they said.

" 'I can give him moral support,' I said.

"Well, they ran to the shelter and I was left alone by Father's bedside, and the bombs started to fall and I was so scared I started to vomit. Strange thing, what fear can do to you and you can't help it. They say most people wet their pants. Well, it was vomiting for your grandma!

"I stood by the bed, with one hand holding my father's hand and with the other—supporting it with my arm, like this—the bedpan. Every time a bomb fell, I vomited. Father would look at me and cry—big awful tears running down his face. He could not speak, as I told you, but with his good hand, he motioned me to leave him and go.

"With the all-clear they came back and I was still holding the pan and vomiting!

"Fine moral support I was! I'm such a coward, Anna. I so admire courage in others."

An epic was written of Aeneas who chose to save his old father over possessions when Troy was being ransacked. It's a well-known moral tale. He risked poverty, not his life, like Grandma. Her story cannot make an epic. She is a simple, unknown woman. Who will ever know of her noble soul? Who will ever know of her courage? She herself does not know.

I STAYED WITH my grandparents for three years. My parents and my baby sister came to visit two or three times a year and, in the summer, as always, we went to Grandpa Damien's country house. I did not miss them. My grandmother had to force me to write them.

"My dearest parents," I wrote. "I eat all my food. I can stand on my head! Daddy, please tell Miss Thompson I don't like to spell. She does not understand me when I tell her. Please. I promise I will learn how to speak only I don't want to learn to spell. Miss Thompson teaches me English. I am a good girl. Grandma is well. I kiss you. Anna."

"My dearest parents. I had the measles. I went fishing with Grandpa. I caught a small fishie. Grandpa caught two big fishes. A swallow made a nest in the veranda. Miss Thompson has a black umbrella. I drew a donkey for Miss Thompson. English donkeys go ih-oh ih-oh like Greek donkeys! I am a good girl. Grandma is well. I kiss you. Anna."

"My dearest parents. Daddy, tell Grandma I don't want to learn piano. Grandma made me a skirt. Grandpa had a toothache. His cheek swelled. The swallow has babies. Miss Thompson gave me a book for my birthday. It has pictures and English. I like the pictures very much. I am a good girl. I kiss you. Anna."

Grandma helped me address the envelopes in my own hand.

"How do the letters get there?"

"You put them in a box."

Any box, I thought. I put a letter in a box and the next day it was still there. Grandma explained it had to be a special box. Grandpa took me down the street and we dropped the letters in the mailbox together. Grandpa also took me to the puppet show and to the park and to the fair and to the movies. We saw American movies. American movies were "appropriate for the underage." European and Greek movies most of the time were marked "inappropriate" with a big red "I." European movies were black and white and had people in them who were like us. American movies were in color and had American people in them. American people in the middle of talking jumped up and sang and danced.

Despite our close companionship and all he did for me, I refused to do anything Grandpa asked of me.

When he worked in the garden, he used to ask, "Anna, my child, move the hose to the next flower bed, so I don't have to get up!"

The watering hose could be by my feet but I said blandly, "No."

Or, he would say, "Go over to the newsstand and buy me a pack of cigarettes—and buy some candy for yourself, too."

I would not even be bribed.

It upset Grandma terribly. "Anna, you are a bad child," she said. "Can't you see Grandpa loves you—all he does for you? Be good to him, child! Be good to him for my sake. It hurts Grandma to see you be bad. It's not right."

I was not dissuaded, only more spiteful that she took his side.

I had gotten in the habit of walking around the house stark naked, though what provoked me to do this I do not remember. My grandfather was puritanical and it shocked him. He was so prudish that he could not bring himself to talk to me and had Grandma approach me.

"Grandpa does not like to see you naked," she said. "You're such a big girl—it's not proper."

This gave me a strong weapon. When I was particularly mean, I sat in front of him naked and opened my legs wide showing off my pee-pee. It made Grandpa furious. He walked out of the room shaking and called out to Grandma, "Ismini, get some clothes on her or I swear I'll kill her!"

I thought it was funny.

Grandma liked looking at my pee-pee. I would say to her, "Grandma, do you want to look at my pee-pee?"

"Let's look at your pee-pee."

I showed her.

"Oooh! Nice pee-pee!" she said.

Grandpa was a stick-in-the-mud not to like it, I thought.

ON ALTERNATE SUNDAYS we went to visit my grandfather's and grandmother's relatives. It was my first entry into the social world, my life till then having been confined to the barracks and stays at my paternal grandfather's house where the moral and intellectual tenets governing life were the same as in our own home—Grandpa Damien, a schoolteacher, and my father, an army officer, being similarly strict and dictatorial. My aunts, the three that remained unmarried and still lived at home, though educated, working women, under their father's indomitable shadow, behaved with the circumspection and the staid decorum of callow schoolgirls.

My grandfather Zisis had two sisters, Theodosia and Efterpi.

Efterpi was the younger of the two. It is said that the first night of her marriage, her husband, a gruff, taciturn man twice her age, had said to her, "What are you waiting for? Take your pants off!" without endearments or preliminaries. She went into shock and never spoke again except in single-word sentences. She had seen her husband only once before, when the marriage was arranged and she brought in to him, with eyes cast down in expected modesty, the customary cup of coffee and glass of water on a tray, so he could look at her face.

When we went to see her, she came to the door and greeted us saying our names, "Zisi . . . Ismini . . . Anna," with solemn benevolence like a benediction, then went back to her chair, where she sat, silent, immobile and impassive, her eyes steadfast in sorrow—a woman meek and dignified, implacably mourning the rape of her virginity, the length of her days. She was dressed in black, her white hair braided around her head like a crown, her face peaceful and unlined, otherworldly in its sad benignity.

She had had five children but only one lived now at home, Lefteris, her last, who had lost his leg in the war and was unemployed. He hobbled around with a crutch, his empty pant leg folded under his stump and fastened with a big safety pin. I watched him with marveling fascination—to my child's mind, a cripple being a rarely encountered, separate species.

They lived in Kastella, near Pireus, and we had to take two buses to get to their house. The protracted anticipation, due to the long, slow trip, spurred my excitement as danger spices adventure. I was to see a mute woman and a one-legged man! Each time we went, I gripped the rail of the bus seat in front of me, intent with delighted expectation.

Theodosia, older and strong-willed, had married a homosexual late in life. The marriage was not consummated. Her husband was now dead, having left her a sizable fortune. She lived with a younger woman, Philio, whom she had taken in as a "soul daughter" and had later legally adopted.

She was an imposing woman, selfish and autocratic, with a caustic, cynical wit and sour temper, tight-fisted and vain. She had a coarse-featured face with mean, deep-set eyes and a mouth turned at the corners, downward with disdain.

Philio was plain and unprepossessing, stout, with a trudging walk, a sensual mouth and vacant, lethargic eyes. She had the humorless, dull-witted gravity of an austere parson.

They lived in a two-story building whose ground floor housed a flower shop. Through a door with panels of cut glass, one walked into a narrow hall that enclosed a winding staircase. There was no light in the hall except what filtered through the entrance.

My grandfather climbed up first, my grandmother following behind, their shadows—his lean and long, hers small and rounded, distorted like a ball—falling on the wall, a fluttering exclamation point to the darkness. Unable to see, I held to the banister. Near the rails, the steps were narrow, precipitously swerving. The well gave me vertigo and I had to move to the outer side, crouching on my hands and knees, dizzy, hugging the wall as a cautious mariner would the shore. It was like this, crawling and trembling, I would first encounter Aunt Theodosia's stern, stately figure towering over me.

With shrunken spirit, I explored the apartment. The curtains were closed to keep out the sun and in the dim light, furniture, floor and walls—lined with wood-paneling halfway up—shone with a dark glimmering glow. The air seemed as though it never moved and smelled of wax and linen doused in lavender.

Only the drawing room, dining room and one bedroom were used. The rest of the rooms were locked. I concluded that Aunt Theodosia and Philio slept in the same room—on the big brass bed whose headrest, forming in the center a wreath of flowers framing two baby angels in embrace, caused me such envy. When they went to the kitchen to prepare our meal, leaving us in the drawing room alone, I said:

"Philio sleeps on the same bed with Aunt Theodosia!"

"Your aunt is an old woman and her feet are cold. She sleeps with Philio to keep them warm," my grandfather said.

Philio lies across the bottom of the bed with her stomach exposed and my aunt rests her feet on it, I thought. I was shocked.

While I was there, I was always shown to the same chair, directly under a chandelier. Convinced it could fall—the thing being immense and suspended by a single cord—I sat with my body at a slant, a strained precarious stance, perched on the edge of my seat, pretending it was a pose.

As Aunt Theodosia disliked children, I was admonished to keep quiet, not to fidget, not to talk. Miserable and scared, I sat in my perilous chair, my body contorted, left out of conversation—chiefly concerned with Aunt Theodosia's symptoms of hypertension, gout and erratic bowel function—ignored, my mind becoming as numb as my body. Boredom—which as a concept or word I did not yet know—was a deadly illness I contracted each time we visited Aunt Theodosia.

I hated her and feared her with the full force of my soul. When she petted my face, it was to see if I was warmer than Philio, I thought. She wanted to ask Grandpa to let me live with her so she could sleep with me instead at night.

This was Grandpa's side of the family.

Grandma's side, more numerous and hale, suave and worldly, gathered every Sunday in the oldest brother's—Uncle Gregoris'—home. This meant two more brothers and three sisters with their husbands and wives, and often their children and grandchildren.

They were affluent and prominent in society, class-conscious, conceited people, blatantly condescending to inferiors. They treated my grandparents with ill-concealed derision, calling my grandfather behind his back "the lord" for his phlegmatic disposition, and my grandmother, the last and favored child of their parents, disparagingly, "Benjamin." They saw her easygoing nature as stemming from frivolity of spirit, her modest simplicity as stupidity. This treatment my grandmother, in her humility, ungrudgingly accepted. To me, who thought her the most wonderful person in the world, their snubbing attitude—to the extent I was sensitive to it—was outrageous, my grandmother's acquiescence to it, a mortification. At those times I felt sympathy and respect for my grandfather, who sat in a corner in Uncle Gregoris' drawing room and, like a dignified spectator at a fatuous show, overbearing and bored, spoke with chilled civility when Grandma's relatives addressed him and otherwise did not utter a word. As the conversation veered to politics, the women following the agitated discussion with a seething silence more fanatical and strident than the men's vocalized passion, my grandfather stared at them impassive. All politicians, he believed, were sui generis corrupt, ideology a mask for self-interest, patriotism a snare for exploiting the rabble's fighting power often to base ends. Good citizenship was good moral conduct, a life led with dignity and respect for the rights of others. When he served in World War I, so he would not take life, he fired his shots in the air—without idealism, without its optimism and faith, standing his ground against futility under fire.

My grandmother, dressed for the occasion in her one good suit, the only new piece of clothing she was able to afford that was in accord with the current fashion, strapped in a corset and wobbly on high heels, sat amidst her family shy and self-effacing, her face peeking under the formality of a hat, her eyes, pools of limpid darkness. Her sisters and sisters-in-law, flamboyant in their finery like bright-plumaged birds, prattled superciliously around her, as adults discounting the mute presence of a child.

The house, bought by proxy when Uncle Gregoris was still living in America where he had emigrated as a young man and come back with fortune and family made, was on a street of "ill repute." The house next door—an elegant, run-down building with marble pediments—was one of Athens' better known brothels. To Uncle Gregoris' great embarrassment, his house was frequently mistaken for it and strange men came knocking at his door at all hours of day and night.

Conversations on Sundays invariably reverted to this problem with yet another tale of some man appearing at the doorstep identifying himself as Zorro, D'Artagnan and, most intriguingly, "The Spigot."

Once my cousin Menelaos, "The Ox," was asked to Uncle Gregoris' house at the instigation of my parents who thought they could make a match between him and one of Uncle's daughters.

Menelaos, who was easily overwrought by social encounters, arrived at the street in trepidation. Absentminded and flustered, he rang next door by mistake. Giving his name as The Ox, he was let in, and found himself in a large hall with women—garishly painted and lewdly dressed—descending on him from all directions. Knowing that Uncle's girls had grown up in America, a country where women were said to be forward and loose, he assumed this was the American way of receiving a suitor and, when one of them began to fondle him, said he would like to get to know her first—and could he pay his respects to her mother?

The story, introduced as "The Ox in the House of Sufferance," was the mainstay of the repertoire, often repeated in front of hapless Menelaos—now engaged to Uncle Gregoris' youngest daughter—who blushed and stammered, "She was about forty, too!"

I asked Zoitsa, who lived at Uncle's with her divorced mother, what a "house of sufferance" was. Zoitsa was eleven.

"It's a bordello," she said.

"I know it's a bordello. What is it though?"

"It's a house God doesn't want men to go to."

"What happens if they go?"

"Their noses fall off, they go crazy and die."

I verified this information with Grandma.

"Do the noses of the men who go to the house next door to Uncle Gregoris' fall off?"

"Sometimes."

"Do they go crazy and die?"

"Sometimes."

"What does sufferance mean?"

Before Grandma could answer, Grandpa said, "Tolerance."

"What does tolerance mean?"

"Let's say I put a pot of water on the stove," he said, "and ask you to put your hand in. The water at first is cold and you do not mind having your hand in it. Then it gets warmer and you still don't mind. Then it gets real hot and hurts a bit but you still can keep your hand in. You can *tolerate* the water. If it hurts so much that you have to take your hand out, you can't *tolerate* the water."

"In the house of sufferance the men who go in feel pain in their nose and more pain and more pain—and they tolerate the pain?"

Grandpa nodded and laughed.

"Do they know they'll lose their nose if they go in?"

"They know."

"How come they go in then?"

"Why do you do something when you know, if you do it, you'll get a spanking?"

In the afternoon, after the big meal when the grown-ups dozed in their chairs and the children were sent upstairs to sleep in beds, I, who could not take naps, went out in the garden.

A stone fence, two meters high, separated the backyards of the two houses. There was a big fig tree next to the wall and, climbing on the tree, I could get on the wall and stand on it. Slowly I would slide my foot over the edge, dangling my leg in the house of sufferance. I had my foot in the garden of the house forbidden by God to enter! I straddled the fence, my left leg in Uncle's house, my right in the house of sufferance, daring apostate, exulting in defiance.

When I heard people stirring inside the house and knew they were waking up, I hurried down and pretended I had been playing, in my deception experiencing a queasy, exhilarating pleasure—the stealthy, insinuating thrill of sin.

When we got back home, Grandma undressed, put on her houserobe and slippers and plopped exhausted in a chair.

I climbed onto her lap like a bounding dog.

"I'm hot and tired, Anna."

I felt angry she did not want me. I kissed and caressed her and did not let up, despite her trying to shake me off.

"Tyrant!" she said. "Tyrant!"

But in the end, she gave up and cuddled me in her arms. We were alone again, she and I, with only Grandpa, watching us wistful but kindly, a reminder of any outside world.

I crouched in her lap, in her love safe and happy. Grandma and I had our own world, I thought. Grandpa's solitary figure, lodged between us, cast a permanent shadow in it, a ray of darkness from the world of other people, alien and fearsome. What did I have to do with that world?

·   ·   ·

I WAS SO ensconced in Grandma's love that when my parents came to claim me, I viewed them as strangers. I knew them, I remembered them, but had no filial feelings for them. Though in awe of my father still, I was no longer the rugged puppet of his will. My grandmother's tenderness and love, her uncritical delight in me and indulgence of my every desire and caprice, had made me selfish and intractable. I had not had to atone for my childish youth as though it were sinful incapacity, as my father had deemed—I had not had to live up to solemnly spelled out standards to be doled out love as reward. Grandma had loved me as I was, no matter what I did. When I misbehaved, she grieved—she did not damn me with anger.

I did not want to leave Grandma. They wrenched me away from her—from the only happiness I had known.

"Don't let them take me away, Grandma!" I begged her, sobbing. "Don't let me go."

"Why, child! They are your parents."

"I don't want to go with them."

"Your grandma loves you more than anything in the world," Grandma said, "but your parents love you even more. They gave you life."

But it was Grandma who had given me life, I thought. I had not been alive before loving Grandma.

"I'll be so lonely without you, Grandma!"

She took a small metal icon down from the icon stand and gave it to me. She said, "Stop crying and I'll tell you the story of Saint Barbara."

I dried my eyes. Grandma put her arms around me, lifted me in her lap and started:

"Saint Barbara was a beautiful, beautiful princess. The people saw her beauty as a sign of God and wherever she went bowed their heads. Her father, the king, was jealous. 'My subjects should bow to me alone,' he said to himself. He shut Saint Barbara in a tower so that the people could not see her.

"Saint Barbara, with God's love, grew even more beautiful in the tower. The king went to see her one day. He went in the tower and what does he see? The guards kneeling at her feet! The king said to himself, 'Her beauty shines on the guards and blinds them to their duty. I'll kill the guards!'

"So the king killed the guards.

"He went back to the tower after one, two—a hundred and two—days and lo! Saint Barbara's beauty was shining in the sun and the sun was bowing to her, lowering his rays at her feet!

"The king said to himself, 'I'll darken out the sun!'

"He summoned his stonemasons and said, 'Go to the tower you built and fill the windows with stone.'

"The stonemasons did as they were told.

"After one, two—a hundred and two—days, the king took a lantern and went to the tower again. For sure, he thought to himself, her beauty in the darkness has died. What did he see, however? The tower was lit inside! There was a bright, bright light—the light of God's love. God bowed to Saint Barbara's beauty!

"The king said to himself, 'The girl is a witch. I'll kill her!'

"He gathered his subjects in the palace yard, had Saint Barbara brought to him, drew his sword and . . ."

"And?"

"*And,* God sent down his lightning and burned him to ashes."

"What happened to Saint Barbara?"

"She lived happily ever after. If you put her icon under your pillow and pray to her every night, she'll love and protect you."

"I want a picture of *you,* Grandma! I want *you* to protect me. Saint Barbara doesn't know me."

"Sure she knows you. She looks down from the sky and can see you. When you feel lonely, pray to her and she'll help you. Saint Barbara helps all little girls who are lonely, as she was lonely in her tower."

I looked at the icon doubtfully. Saint Barbara had deep, sunken, austere eyes and thin, unsmiling stiff lips. I did not like her looks. She was not blond like a princess, either.

"I want a picture of you, too," I said.

In my parents' home, I put the icon and Grandma's picture under my pillow side by side. At night, when I kissed the icon, Saint Barbara's cold metal face chilled my lips and I could not pray. If God loved Saint Barbara why did He let her father imprison her? Why didn't He kill him before he had her put in the tower? Why did He let her be lonely? I thought.

I kissed Grandma's picture, stared at it disconsolately, crying. Night after night I cried myself to sleep. With time, the picture became tear-stained, tattered with my grief, the face on it a gray scary blur.

My Father's Daughter

I HAVE A picture of my father and myself published in a newspaper. The caption reads, "Man Carrying Child Crosses the Narrows of Euripus." My father is swimming on his side. He holds a rope in his teeth. The other end of the rope is tied around the inner tube from a tire. I'm hanging inside the tube, my face small, barely visible. I must be about two. I stare over the tube's rim thoughtfully, my eyes hurtful, earnest. They show no fear but fatalism, profound sadness and sagacity—yet the mouth smiles at the camera with pleading, helpless innocence.

My father was a student at the Chalkida Military School at the time. He had trained to cross the channel all summer. The water in the narrows runs for six hours north and for six hours south, with the inflow and outflow of the tide. As the current changes direction, the undertow becomes treacherous. The small boats that cross the channel back and forth stay anchored at the shore and the sea is empty. Every evening at this time, he swam against the current, taking me with him—a man testing his endurance, a small child in a tire bobbing in his wake like flotsam.

I do not remember this from experience. My father often repeated the story to friends in later years, roaring with laughter as he added, "Old Mavros was on the drawbridge once and saw me. He's a brigadier general now—he was colonel then. 'You'll drown the child, Karystine!' he hollered. 'You'll drown the child.' "

When I was nine, the summer I went back home after living with my grandparents, he was stationed in Chalkida

again, a teacher at the military school this time. The first
day, he took me to these same waters to teach me how to
swim.

Raising my body with his hands under my stomach, he
said, "Relax and you'll float. Move your arms about."

I was told to float and I floated.

He took his arms away and said, "Now, swim!"

I swam.

He taught me the different strokes and how to flip on my
back when I was tired. "You don't need to touch bottom to
rest," he said. "You can go as far out in the sea, as you like.
You must know your own strength. Think beforehand, 'If I
go that far out, will I be able to swim back?' "

There was no lifesaver now, no rope. Connecting me to
him, ever stronger, was the power of his will. His presence
clamped around my heart like an iron brace. It did not dis-
place Grandma's love, but it blackened it, snuffing out the
last glimmer of happiness I had felt living with her.

I read all day in my room, door and shutters closed
because the glare of the sun hurt my eyes. I read in darkness,
kneeling on the floor, a book propped on the edge of my bed,
slowly sliding my finger beneath each word.

People in books were unhappy, as I was, but their unhappiness was beautiful, I thought. The more a book made me
cry, the more I loved it. Books did not have an autonomous
existence, I realized. Behind each book I could feel a live
presence, the writer, his voice vibrant in my mind's ear. Even
when a character died at the end, the voice was still alive. It
was like magic.

I want to write, too, I thought. If I write my suffering
down in a book, it will become beautiful. I tried to write but
my hand moved slowly and it tired me. My mind was too
fast for my hand. I'll have to wait till I grow up and can write
faster, I thought.

I wrote poems, however. Poems were short. They were not about suffering, my poems. They were like songs. They came to my mind as a tune. I wrote down the words and all by themselves they rhymed. I wrote a poem about the lemon tree in the yard and one about a centipede and one about the Greek flag.

I recited them for Mama.

"Aha!" said my godfather. "A budding artist."

My godfather, Leandros, was a painter. He had rented the house next to ours, Chalkida being a resort, and with my father's fortuitous stationing there, he thought it a good opportunity for them all to be together.

He was chunky and bald, a garrulous, free-spirited man, with a roguish incivility that endeared him to women and amused the men. He had been my father's best friend since childhood.

My father used to say to him, "Who would have thought you would turn out an artist? Had I only known, Leandre! Now here I am, stuck—my best friend an artist!"

Both men laughed.

He painted pictures with muddled outlines, broad, coarse strokes of jarring colors and called them, "Ostrich Saluting Danger," "Stone, Patient" and "Uranium." He was working on another called "Euripus' Suicide," a blur of blues and yellows. I knew from school Euripus had killed himself, drowning in the waters now bearing his name, because he could not explain why the current in the channel, every six hours, changed. I thought I could not understand the picture because it was not finished yet. When one day he said it was done, my father and I went to see it.

It looked no different.

My godfather tried to explain his picture. "It's what you see," he said.

"Where is Euripus?"

"It's his spirit I've painted."

"His spirit is blue and yellow?"

My godfather laughed. "We Greeks were the first people to puzzle over and try to explain the mystery of the world— to make science out of primitive wonder," he said. "First of all peoples, we posited reason. We tried to explain the workings of the world through logic. Do you know what logic is?"

"Yes, but I don't know how to say it."

"Look at my shoes. They are muddy. Why are they muddy?"

"Because there's mud on them."

"Why is there mud on them?"

"Because there's mud outside and you stepped on it."

"Why is there mud outside?"

"Because it rained."

"Now, this is logical thinking: The mind asks, 'Why are Godfather's shoes muddy?' Logic answers, 'Godfather came in from outside. If there is mud on his shoes, there must be mud outside. If there's mud outside, it must have rained. Therefore, Godfather's shoes are muddy because it rained.' "

I had known that without thinking! Nevertheless, I pursued with the same method: Why did it rain? Because there were rain clouds in the sky. Why were there rain clouds in the sky? Because we had bad weather. Why did we have bad weather? Because God was angry. Godfather's shoes were muddy because God was angry!

"There you have it," Godfather said. "Euripus. He could not explain the tide logically. He knew the moon caused it. But *why?* It defied reason.

"Men have killed themselves despairing over love, men have killed themselves despairing over life, and a Greek kills himself over the limits of reason! That's pride, Annio. Hear me? That's *pride!*"

He pointed at the painting. "That's what I've tried to say here," he said. "With colors."

"I see. Blue is for the sea and yellow for pride."

"You get ten in Logic and zero in Art, Anna," my father said, laughing. Then addressing my godfather, "For a while there I was scared you might have passed artistic sensibility on to her—along with the baptismal oil."

"She may surprise you yet. 'Mars's child is Apollo's stepchild.' "

"Eat your tongue, Leandre!"

A few days later, coming unexpectedly in my room, my father found me reading *Lassie, Come Home* and crying. He grabbed the book away from my hands and slapped me.

"That should give you cause for crying," he said. "Blubbering like a moonstruck idiot! Reading sentimental trash! And I who praised your mind! Get out of my sight!"

For days after this incident, he did not speak to me. When I was in the same room with him, he ignored me, not deigning to even show me his contempt. This vengeful silence, spiteful and calculated, much meaner punishment than a whipping, he prolonged at will. He did not love me anymore, I thought. Never again would he love me. I was a weakling, unworthy of him. I did not deserve his esteem. Who, what, was I, if my father treated me as though I did not exist?

One day, in late afternoon, as he and my godfather were getting ready to go to the beach, he turned to me and said, "Put on your swimsuit!"

I ran to my room and changed. When I came out, they had left.

"Mama, do you think Daddy meant I should go along?"

"Yes," she said. "Run! Go."

Her anxious voice flowed through me like a chill. She's frightened for me, I thought. Why? Why is she frightened?

She came with me to the door, opened it and, stepping aside from the cascade of sunlight suddenly flooding the room, stood in the shadow, her beautiful face desolate, her silence the muteness of a life smothered by futile longing, her inexpressible love, her shackled joy.

She watched from the house as I ran to meet my father, her worried eyes boring into my back, pushing me toward panic. I ran faster.

When I got to the beach, my father and Godfather Leandros were already in the water. I sat on their towel and waited. I was afraid my father might not want me in the water with him. When he came out, he said, "Well, go in! Don't you want to swim?"

He gave me a push to make me stand up and smiled. He has forgiven me, I thought. Just like that!

I ran in the sea and, overjoyed, swam, far out to the deep, then turned around and treaded water, looking back at the beach. My father and my godfather sat on the sand, smoking and talking, their wet hair tousled in the breeze. The blue, gleaming water surrounded me, still and serene, enclosing me in its beauty, wistful as in a dream. My father looked up and waved, then lay down on his back. Suddenly, the keen absolving joy I had felt when I first dove in the water drained from me. I felt empty inside, a heavy emptiness, weighing me down. The sea began to ripple—gently, caressingly on the surface, churning with treachery underneath. The current is changing, I thought. I started to swim back, frantic. For every stroke I went forward, I was drawn two back, or so it seemed.

"The tide's coming on!" I screamed.

My godfather jumped up and ran toward the sea. My father ran after him. He fell on him, holding him back. They fought, then moved apart, my father standing at the edge of the water, my godfather a little behind him. My godfather's face was slack with anxiety, my father's rigid, stern.

I must not show fear, I thought. I beat on the water with my arms as I swam, beating my fear to death. My fear made me want to live. I had to live to kill my fear. I swam harder, with all my might. I no longer thought or felt anything. When my feet touched bottom and I could wade, my body started to shake. It continued to shake, even after I was out of the water.

"You are inhuman, Stephane," my godfather said to my father.

"If every time a toddler stumbles you catch him, he'll never walk. She's a good swimmer."

" 'It's the good swimmer who drowns.' "

"Yes. And: 'The mother of the brave shall mourn.' I know all the proverbs. You know what I say? What I learned in the war: You are a man or you are cannon fodder."

"She's a girl, Stephane."

"A girl! She's my daughter! She's my pride."

" 'Pride comes before a fall.' "

"It seems to me I've heard from your very lips an oration about the Greek spirit—about our reason and pride."

"It's been our undoing."

"Our glory," my father said, bending to pick up his cigarettes lying on the beach. Seeing the pack was empty, he walked over to the kiosk on the sidewalk to buy another one, then came back. He put his arm around me.

My father thinks I'm brave—I swam ashore, I thought. I must always be brave, so my father stays proud.

"It's time we head home," he said.

My godfather followed, a few steps behind.

Every day from then on, I swam farther and farther out—farther than anyone else swam—out to the deep where the water held Euripus' haunted soul. I was exhilarated. I was swimming in Euripus' proud spirit. I was swimming out where the waters, reaching back beyond memory, drenched in history, were immortal.

Printed in the United States
by Baker & Taylor Publisher Services